The Letters
a carnage novella

by
LESLEY JONES

Copyright 2016 Lesley Jones
All Rights Reserved

This is a work of fiction. Any references to real events, real people, and real places are used fictitiously. Other names, characters, places and incidents are products of the Author's imagination and any resemblance to persons, living or dead, actual events, organisations or places is entirely coincidental.

All rights are reserved. This book is intended for the purchaser of this e-book ONLY. No part of this book may be reproduced or transmitted in any form or by any means, graphic, electronic, or mechanical, including photocopying, recording, taping, or by any information storage retrieval system, without the express written permission of the Author. All songs, song titles and lyrics contained in this book are the property of the respective songwriters and copyright holders.

Editing by Ash Williams @ http://www.awediting.com/

Cover design & Formatting by Rebel Edit & Design

Cover image Copyright 2016

ACKNOWLEDGMENTS

I will keep these short and simple.

Firstly my family, thank you for your patience and understanding. I know that I'm not easy to live with when I'm writing, which is constantly lately, so thank you for putting up with my crap and the absences when I travel to meet my readers. I love you and I think they do too.

To my PA Jen and her husband Tai, thanks for everything you do, but mainly the friendship.

Thank you to my beautiful Beta's and my amazing admin teams for keeping my world running smoothly.

Thanks to my editor Ash, I will have speaking proper English soon my luv, I promise.

To my readers. My readers, what can I say about you lot? You're passion never ceases to amaze me, thank you, thank you for loving these characters and all their flaws.

To Margreet, for another perfect cover. You just 'get' me every single time.

To all of the bloggers that have ever given me a mention, I have a career, because of you lot.

Thank you everyone that has loved Georgia since she was eleven years old, for staying with her through the years, her loves, her losses, her laughs and her tantrums. Thank you for loving Sean, Cam, Marley and all of the Layton's. These characters have consumed my life for two and a half years and now it's time to say goodbye.

That's it, short and sweet, just like me ☺

DEDICATION

For my readers.
You asked.
I hope I delivered.

TABLE OF CONTENTS

ACKNOWLEDGMENTS	5
DEDICATION	7
TABLE OF CONTENTS	9
CHAPTER 1	11
CHAPTER 2	21
CHAPTER 3	29
CHAPTER 4	37
CHAPTER 5	45
CHAPTER 6	51
CHAPTER 7	61
CHAPTER 8	81
CHAPTER 9	91
CHAPTER 10	113
EPILOGUE	129
PLAYLIST	137
AUTHOR BIO	139
ALSO BY LESLEY JONES	141

CHAPTER 1

I clear customs in record time. The upside of landing at two in the morning I suppose. I am tired and miserable and just want to get home. As I enter the arrivals hall, I scan the space for my driver, who should be holding up a card with my name on it. I could've called Benny but thought I'd spare him the task. He hasn't been well lately, blood pressure and a dodgy knee are both causing him problems. I'd paid for him to start working out with a personal trainer three times a week, and as much as he moaned about it, he has lost over three stone this last six months, and I know he is feeling better for it.

I spot a bloke of about thirty, holding up a card with my name on it and looking right at me. I do my best to keep my name out of the papers as much as possible, but he obviously recognises me. Giving him a small tilt of my chin in acknowledgment, I head around the barrier, dragging my suitcase behind me.

I could use the company's private jet to travel, but it seems like such a waste for just one person, so I fly first class instead. No hardship there.

"Mr King, let me take that for you, sir," my driver says as I reach him. "My name's Parker, sir. I'll be your driver tonight." I give him another nod and let him take my case as I contemplate cracking a joke and asking him to call me Lady Penelope, seeing as his name is Parker. Like I said, though, it's two in the morning, and I am not particularly cheerful right now.

"If you'd like to follow me, sir, we'll get you settled in the car and home in no time."

I remain silent and follow him to the Jag that is gonna get me home. Home to my Kitten and my kids. I hate being away and rarely make trips without Georgia, but this one was too important for me not to attend. We have one club in Australia, one in Asia, and four clubs throughout Europe now, and this week I had to meet with the heads of security for each one. Gone are the days of trying to stop underage kids with fake IDs, hidden miniature bottles of alcohol, or drugs in shoes. Now, the staff are searching for guns and suicide bombers. The world is a scary place and nightclubs are not immune to terrorists or rampaging idiots with guns. Our clubs are all upmarket and frequented by celebrities, as well as average clubbers, and I want each and every one of them to feel safe. The meetings over the last two weeks were about upgrading all of our systems and brainstorming best practices. It was far from exciting but very necessary. On any given weekend, my clubs are filled with other people's children, and I have a duty of care to each and every one of them. One day, my kids would be off out clubbing, well, not until they are at least thirty, of course, for my daughters it may be never! But anyway, when that time comes, I want the standards of club security to be at a lot higher level than they were when I first started out.

My kids.

I couldn't even think the words without smiling.

Two boys and two girls.

Those four little people and their mother are my world. One I never thought I would have with anyone, let alone their mother. My Kitten. The absolute love of my life

We'd taken a long and winding road, with unimaginable loss and heartbreak along the way, to get to each other, but we got here. Middle-aged and the happiest and most content we'd ever been in our lives.

We have been beyond fortunate to have brought four beautiful babies into this world as a bonus. Four little people that grow every day into young adults. Harry, who is fifteen now, is all legs, exactly the way I was when I was his age. We got lucky with that kid. As sad as it is to say, I'm relieved he has none of Tamara's personality traits. H is generally the mediator amongst the kids. He's pretty calm and easy going and no one would guess he is only a few months older than the rest of the kids, since he acts like an adult already. He is in the year above them at school and made sure everyone knew not to even think about breathing in the direction of his sisters, let alone looking at them when they joined him at secondary school they all attend. He steps in between their fights, which are frequent, and he helps them with their homework. He rarely argues with his brother or gives us any lip. He knows his background and that Georgia isn't his birth mother. She's the only mum he's ever known, and since the day he came to live with us, that's all he's ever called her. I'll admit that I was a little worried that her feelings might changes towards Harry when George and the twins arrived. That never happened, and the older he gets, the closer they seem to become. He goes to his mum for everything, and I mean everything. Hair product, girl advice, what T-shirt to wear to the shopping centre, all Georgia. The little shit never asks my advice on anything, his usual response to anything I say, is, "Get with it, old man". He even sends her pictures of things before he buys them. I mean seriously, if you can't dress yourself by the age of fifteen, then what fucking hope is there for the kids of today?

I watch the lights of the A13 pass by as we head away from City Airport and back towards Essex, to my home, my wife, my children, my world.

By the time I walk through my front door, it's almost four in the morning. I need to be inside my wife. One week is far too long to go without feeling her skin against mine. I've gone beyond tiredness by this stage, so I head straight through the house towards the kitchen. I'll have a coffee and some toast and then go wake my wife up with coffee with my extra special cream and a kiss … from my dick.

I take my shoes off so they don't make noise on the hardwood floor. I'm home a day and a half early, and I don't wanna be scaring the crap outta Georgia.

Walking down the hallway towards our family room, I pass my office first and then Georgia's. We tried sharing, but I find her too untidy and distracting. Every time she leant forward or bent over, I'd end up fucking her and neither of us ever got any work done. I ended up moving the gym out to the pool house and turning the extra room into a separate office for Georgia. I had it soundproofed, too. Georgia likes to listen to music when she works, I like silence.

I stop in my tracks and take a step back as I see a light shining from the slightly open door to my wife's office. Still holding my shoes in my hand, I push the door open slowly and take a look inside.

Georgia's office is the complete opposite of mine. Where I have a huge wooden desk facing the door, Georgia has a deep ledge against the window that she works from with her back *to* the door. My walls have a couple of pieces of art I've collected over the years by Peter Granville Edmunds and my bookshelves have pictures of Georgia, myself, and the kids on them.

Georgia's office furniture is made from what looks like drift wood, she has one wall painted with a pop art looking piece. It's black and white and divided into squares. Each square is a continuation of the picture in the adjoining square. In the centre is a re-joined image of us kissing, around the edges are pictures of the kids. It sounds like a complicated mess, but the impact knocks my breath away every time I step into the room. On the opposite wall, she has the kids' heights marked out, starting from the time they could stand. The rest of the wall is covered in ours and the kid's handprints, and each one has something written in the palm: Love. Trust. Live. Family. Laugh. Be kind. Be honest to yourself. I love you all are just some of the words and phrases that jump out at me. Every time I look at this wall it gives me a lump in my throat. On the walls on either side of the door are the gold, silver, and platinum awards Carnage has won over the years, and on the shelves on either side of the window where her desk sits are the awards she's won for all of her charity work, framed photos of us and the kids, and drawings the kids have made for her. Her office is all family, mine more professional-looking, which sometimes makes me feel like a bit of an old fart.

Georgia's office is never tidy, but right now, the mess is off the charts. There's what looks like an old tea chest, or packing crate sitting in the corner and piles of documents and books on every surface. I look at the floor, and my heart rate speeds up when I see her.

Kitten.

She's lying flat on the floor in a pair of shorts and an old Carnage T-shirt. Her hair is piled on top of her head, and she has her pink Beats covering her ears.

She has a piece of paper pressed against her chest, and she's crying. She makes no sound, there are no facial expressions, just tears. They track from the corners of her eyes, into her ears, around her neck, and into her hairline.

I fight the urge to go to her, to sweep her up and hold her tightly in my arms. To rock her and tell her to hush, that everything will be all right, because it won't.

She's crying for him. Her lost love.

She's crying for them. Her lost babies.

And there's nothing I can do or say to make it better.

There was a time when I would have gladly taken their places. When I would've given my life for theirs just to bring the light back into her eyes, but not now. Now, I'm a dad. Sacrificing myself for them would mean my, *our* children, wouldn't exist. So, now I say nothing when she has her bad days. I just reassure her that she's not a bad person.

Does it hurt? Of course it fucking does. I'm only human.

I'm always aware of when Georgia is having her bad days. I know that there's a part of her that will forever mourn Sean and the babies they lost. I know my girl, though, and I know without a shadow of a doubt that even when she cries for them, she loves me with everything she has.

I'd be a fucking liar if I say I don't feel just a little stab of jealousy when she has her meltdown moments and cries for the loss of another man—a man she loved with all her heart until she met me and gave me a piece of it too. A man she left me for and went on to marry. A man she cheated on with me when she let me fuck her senseless against my office door. A man she refused to leave so we could be together. I learnt a long time ago that being jealous of a dead bloke is futile and a complete waste of energy.

I know Georgia struggles with her guilt, and I understood that. Yet, neither of us could change the tragic events that afflict our pasts; twisted, bent, and moulded our futures; and then ultimately led us back to each other. What I can do is hold her when she cries and reassure her it is okay to let the tears flow. She loved him for most of her life and it is okay to still love him now to cry for her loss.

I knew when I married her there would always be a piece of her heart I could never mend. A piece that will always belong to them, but it's part of what makes her Georgia, and I wouldn't change her for the world. We both had to kick, bite, and claw our ways from the deepest depths of hell to find what we have now. It was hard, but we did it—against the odds, we fucking did it.

My wife turns onto her side and pulls her knees up to her chest as she gives out a sob. I don't know what she's listening to, as the music is being Bluetoothed from her laptop to her ear phones, but I would bet my arse it's either one of his songs or something that reminds her of him.

I contemplate just leaving her to it and not interrupting what should have been a private moment. She's not expecting me until tomorrow lunch time and will be mortified to know I saw her like this.

I hear a door creek upstairs and turn my attention towards it. The last thing I want is for one of the kids to come down and find her in this state. I take the stairs two at a time and see Kiki heading into my room.

"Kiks?" I call her name quietly, not wanting to wake the other three.

She turns and looks at me over her shoulder and her face lights up.

"You all right, Treacle?" I ask her as she steps into my open arms.

"I thought you weren't coming home till tomorrow? We missed you," she tells me, whilst wrapping her arms around my waist.

I breathe in the scent of her hair, long and deep. She smells like home. I kiss the top of her head and then tilt it so she's looking at me.

"What you doing up?"

"I had a bad dream," she tells me, not meeting my eyes.

"The same one?"

She nods her head.

Before Harry started at secondary school, we sat him down and told him what happened to his mum. He was eleven and had access to the internet, so we thought we needed to do it before some little arsehole at school got in before we did. There was a fair bit of publicity around Tamara's suicide, mainly because she tried to take me out with her and that only made the news because of my relationship with Georgia. To this day, the press and the public seem to have a fascination with my wife. We've managed to protect the kids from it, but they are fully aware I was shot and that their mum was married to someone famous before me. They know the circumstances of his death and about the two babies Georgia lost.

If it were my call, I would've waited until they were older, but as my kids keep telling me, this is the twenty-first century. One click and the kids would've found out the truth, or a version of it, so we decided to be upfront and honest with them. We told H about his mum first and then we told the other three about Tamara and about Sean.

They took it okay, well, sorta. Kiks cried because it was so sad Tamara chose to leave Harry in that way. Lu mumbled something about it being a good thing she had died, otherwise *she* would be hunting her down and shooting Tamara herself. George just asked me if it hurt.

Unfortunately, since then, Kiki has had nightmares. They don't happen often, but they're always about the same thing: either someone is chasing her with a gun, or she's involved in a car accident.

We both feel guilty about this and still wonder if we'd made a bad call telling them all too soon. Then, when Lu got in a fight because some little darling said her mum told her that Georgia was in the papers for having a threesome with some rock stars when she was just thirteen, we knew we had made the right decision.

Being a parent is tough, toughest job I've ever had. I do what I can to protect them, but at the same time I have to prepare them for the outside world. For our kids, it is always gonna be a little bit harder out there, both their mum and their uncle have lived their lives making headlines from a very young age. They have one cousin in an up-and-coming band and another whose face is plastered on billboards, the front of magazines, and sometimes on the telly. Even I have made the front pages a few times.

They have laptops and smart phones. We didn't allow them to have Facebook accounts until they got to secondary school, but now they have it all—Facebook, Twitter, Periscope, Snapchat, and Instagram. There are probably others I don't even know about; the whole thing is beyond me. What ever happened to just knocking on your mate's door and asking if they want to come out?

We have a strict no phones at the dinner table rule, and the only time it gets broken is when they all start taking photos of their food before they start to eat. What the fuck is that all about? I'm glad Georgia is the one in charge of watching their online shit and not me.

Georgia is all over the social media shit and she regularly checks the kids accounts to see what they're looking at, but she's warned me that it is gonna have to stop soon, especially with Harry. She trusts him and says he is entitled to his privacy. Yeah, we'll see.

I walk Kiks back to her bed and lie down with her for a little while. She's the sensitive one out of all my kids. She always used to rescue lady birds and any other creature she found in the garden when she was younger. She cries if a sad story comes on the news, and she donates part of her allowance every month to the local animal shelter.

"So, you missed me, did ya, Treacle?"

She nods her head and yawns at the same time.

"We all missed you. Mum's been sad all week. We watched your wedding video the other night, and she cried all the way through."

My heart bangs so hard against my chest, it echoes in my ears. Most people don't see the gentler side of Georgia. They see the smart business woman that runs a successful chain of fashion stores and an even more successful charity. They see a woman that overcame the very public loss of her first baby and then her husband and a second child. Georgia's public persona is that of a tough-as-nails, smart-mouthed Essex girl. Me, our children, and her family know different. The kids laugh when she cried when Harry scored his first goal and when Kiki was an angel in the school's Christmas play. They have no clue why she cries when she hears the national anthem sung before a football match or when certain songs come on the radio. They don't understand why she cries when someone gets voted off X Factor, or why she bursts into tears when I come home with flowers for her, just because.

But I know.

I know Georgia inside out. From the twenty-year-old girl with sad eyes who walked into my wine bar almost thirty years ago, to the stunningly beautiful, mostly vibrant woman she is now, I know her like no other. Every tear, gasp, and sigh. Every curve, bump, and crease. Every twitch of her lips and thought that crosses her mind, I know and can read them. We talk without words. I can look at her and know when someone is making her uncomfortable, when she's had too much to drink and it's time to go, or when someone's pissing her off and it's time to step in. I know all of this because we're a team, united. There is so much more to her than the public could ever conceive.

"Mum looked so beautiful in her wedding to you. I like that dress better than the one she wore to her other wedding."

"Me too, Treacle, me too."

"Hope I'm as beautiful as her when I grow up." She yawns her way through her sentence. I kiss the top of her head again.

"You already are. Don't you worry about that. You, your sister, and your mum are the best looking girls in the world."

She nods her head, her eyes now closed.

"Ollie Chalmers said that me and Lu were the fittest twins he's ever known, but it's not surprising coz our mum's a MILF."

What the actual fuck?

I'm paying six grand a term, per kid, to send my girls to a school where they get told shit like this? I'll be on the phone with that stuck-up headmistress first thing Monday morning, and who the fuck is this Ollie kid anyway?

"How old is this Ollie kid, Kiks? Do the boys know him?" I choke out because I've forgotten to breathe. She doesn't answer, so I give her a nudge.

"Whaaaat?" she whines.

"This Ollie, how old?"

"Same age as us, fourteen he's in the same tutor group as George, and they play in the same football team."

He's only fourteen, but I still wanna punch the little fucker.

I listen to my daughter's breathing change as she drifts back to sleep.

"I love you," she mumbles

I kiss her forehead this time.

"Love you, too."

I climb from her bed, and as I reach the door, she calls my name.

"Daddy?"

My heart feels like it grows too big for my chest. That shit never gets old. No matter how big of a man I think I am, when my little girl calls me daddy, game over.

"Yes?"

"You looked very handsome in your wedding video … Mum said so, too."

"Thanks, Kiks," I tell her with a smile.

CHAPTER 2

Cameron

I make my way downstairs quietly, the sun is coming up and the birds are starting their dawn chorus. I wanna shoot them.

I was a fourteen-year-old boy once, I know exactly how their filthy little minds work. I need to get Harry on board with this, and make sure he tells that little toerag Ollie to stay the fuck away from my girls—all of them. What the fuck is he doing eyeing up my wife anyway? He's fourteen for fuck's sake.

I take a few deep breaths and stick my head inside Georgia's office door. Her earphones are off and she's curled on her side facing me now, obviously asleep. Her mouth is slightly open, and I'm instantly hard as I watch her.

I go to the kitchen and make us both a coffee. Taking them back to her office, I put them down on her desk next to the two empty bottles of wine I failed to spot earlier. No wonder she was such a mess. Georgia, wine, and memories of Sean are really not a good combination and nearly always end in tears.

There's a stack of letters sitting next to the empty bottles, and I pick the top one up. It's addressed to Georgia when she still lived at home with her parents. I lean over her to make sure she's still sleeping and slide the letter from the envelope.

Oh shut up, like you wouldn't have a look!

It's handwritten on a plain piece of paper.

Let Me Know...
Should I wait for you?
Or let you go
Shall I hang on to our love

I need to know.

My heart, it's yours
For as long as we live
It beats fierce and strong
And has so much to give.
Just let me know…

Fuck!

I know what this is. Georgia has had a crate of stuff sitting out in the garage for years. It had all of Sean's stuff in there, including a load of shit she never looked at. Letters, tapes, diaries. She has always put off going through it, obviously, she's decided now would be a good time to make a start.

I slide the first note back into its envelope and pull out another.

I fucked someone else tonight, George. I hope you're happy with that! Hope you're pleased, hope it's what you wanted, coz I just feel like shit. It didn't have to be like this. It shouldn't have been her who woke up in my bed this morning, it should've been you. It should be you every morning, but you chose this. You chose to behave like a spoiled selfish little cunt, and now I've gone and done exactly what you accused me of in the beginning. Well fuck you, Georgia. Fuck you!

Shit! It should make me happy that Archangel Sean wasn't quite as perfect as Georgia seems to think he was, but this will break her heart. No wonder she was such a mess earlier.

I go into my study and get a throw from the wingback chair I have in there. She's gonna have a stiff neck and a sore head when she wakes up, so the least I can do is keep her warm.

I drink my coffee, as well as the one I made her, and decide to keep reading. I don't care if she's gonna be pissed off with me later. If she's been through all of these and they've upset her, then I wanna know about it. If they're full of poncy words and bullshit, I wanna know that too. What can I say, I'm a nosey fucker, and if it involves my wife, I wanna know it all.

I slide down on the floor next to Georgia and start with the pile that's next to her.

So what now, G? I just give up? You think by ignoring my calls and letters that's it, the end of us? Coz that will never fucking happen. Ignore me all you like, marry someone else, have ten kids with him, it won't matter. There'll still be an us. There'll always be an us.

That looks like anus haha and don't marry anyone else. Fuck, don't even go out with anyone else, and definitely don't have any kids. Beau and Lilly remember? Our babies, G. The babies we're gonna have. We still have to think of a name for our other boy. I was thinking about it the other night, what about Frankie? I think your dad would like that. Beau, Frankie, and Lilly, our kids. Mine and yours.

Fuck, I miss you so fucking much. I don't know what I can say to fix this. I fucked up, I know I fucked up massively, but this is us, we're talking about, Sean and Georgia. Georgia and Sean. We're meant to be, baby, wherever you are, whatever you're doing, there'll always be an us, and you know it. You fucking know it, G.

Why won't you just talk to me?
Ok, don't even do that, just answer the phone when I call and let me talk, just let me tell you how much I love and miss you. Your smell, your touch, your soft skin, and those beautiful blue eyes. Your mouthy Essex attitude, even your temper, G, and your tits—fuck, I miss your tits, your perfect, perfect tits. Every part of me aches. My heart, my soul, and my bones, they all ache for you, baby, so much, so, so much.

I have to go now. We're in Birmingham, Jimmie's here with Len. You should be here with me, and you fucking know it.

I love you, I miss you. I'll call you tomorrow morning around 8 after your dad's gone. Pick up the phone, G. Please, please pick up the phone.

I love you Gia, with everything I am, I love and miss you. Just pick up the phone and talk to me baby. Let me put this right.

Sean xxx

Georgia, Georgia give us a kiss
Georgia, Georgia show us ya tits.
That's all I've got.
Just wanted ya to know that I'm thinking of you.
Love and miss you baby xxx

Georgia, today has been really hard. We're in our new shared house near the studios in West London. We had a day off today, and everyone has gone out, except me. I had nowhere to go. This is where I live, but it's not my home. It's the place where I eat and sleep. Where I shower and wash my clothes. It's where I exist, barely, but it's not my home. My only home is wherever you are. Home is you, the taste of you, the feel of you, the smell of you.

Today, I spent alone. Today, like all the others lately, I spent homeless, because without you, that's what I'll always be.

I love you, Gia. You know that, it never changes, not even when I think I hate you. Even then, I know deep, deep down that it's just another way of loving you. I hope you read this one day. I hope you read this and finally understand, finally get it. Xxx

I wrote a new song, but your brothers, yeah, two of them and your best friend weren't impressed, and I got a punch in the mouth off all of them. I might just make it anyway. I might just go solo on this one and put it out there by myself, what d'ya reckon?

What should I call it? I was thinking "A Song for G", or how about "Fuck You, Baby". How's that sound?

You called this on.
Now you've got your way.
Time for me to move along.
Tomorrow's another day.
Fuck you, baby, I did my best
Fuck you, baby, now I'll go fuck the rest.

I tried to reason, to make you see sense
But you walked away ... No recompense.
You gave me no chance to talk or say my sad goodbyes

You ignored my pleas, ignored my cries.
So fuck you, baby, now I'll go fuck the rest.
I fucked you baby ... You weren't the best.

When you meet another, which I'm sure you will.
Just remember me and the way I can make you feel.
When he slides inside you, and when he holds you tight,
I hope you think and dream of me, all through the night.
When he pushes deep and looks into your cold hard eyes.
When he says and does those things only I know you like,
Don't you forget that I was your first, the first to hear your moans, the first to make you sighs.

So, fuck you, baby. My time here is done.
I'm through crying, time for me to have some fun.
Fuck you, baby, maybe see you around some time.
Then you can join all the others and wait your turn in line.
You like that? Hurts doesn't it? Well good. At least if it hurts, it means you still have a heart. If it weren't for this permanent pain, this continuous ache I have in my chest, I'd be numb. I've got nothing else right now, G. I'm done.

My heart races as I read. I switch from totally understanding the bloke's heartbreak to wanting to smash his face in. Then I remember that he's dead and getting pissed off with him is pointless. I don't understand why she's putting herself through this. It's been fifteen years, why would she want to drag up all of these memories now?

I look down and watch Georgia sleep. As much as I like to think I know what makes her tick, I'd still love to get inside her head sometimes. Like now, just so I can understand the thought process that led to her believing this could be a good idea.

My eyes are starting to sting, and I decided to wrap myself around my wife and rest them for a little while.

CHAPTER 3

Cameron

After what feels like just five minutes of sleep, I wake with a start. I open my eyes and see Georgia lying in the recovery position next to me. Her side pressed into mine as I lie on my back. I hear quiet footsteps walk past the study and on into the kitchen. I assume it's one of the kids but get up anyway to check.

At some stage, I must have taken off my jeans, as I'm now just wearing a T-shirt and a pair of boxers. Georgia stirs and so does my dick as I hear her little sigh. I adjust what's happening inside my Calvin's, collect the glass things Georgia insists we drink our coffee out of, and head up the hallway.

Tallulah is standing at the coffee machine with her head resting on her arms, which are resting on the kitchen worktop. Her long dark hair, which is the exact same shade as her mother's hair, is hanging down her back, and she's watching the hot dark liquid fill her cup.

When the fuck did my daughter start drinking coffee?

Tallulah is probably going to be our problem child. She has a short fuse and a quick wit. She can cut with a glare from her blue eyes or a single word from her sharp tongue. She's also loyal, possessive, and protective of those she loves. Lu has no fear, and her strong will and defiance have already gotten her into trouble. She takes no shit from anyone—not even her teachers, and I've had to go up to the school on more than one occasion. She's not naughty, per se, just outspoken, fearless, and headstrong. She's a passionate kid. I don't wanna sound like I'm making excuses for her, but I don't want the system to knock her spirit out of her. Despite what life has thrown at Georgia, she still maintains hers to this day. In fact, it's what I think got her through everything. I want Lu to grow up to be as resilient as her mum. I want that for all of my kids.

The problem at home is that Lu and Georgia are a fucking nightmare when they start going at each other. Their personalities are identical, and when they clash, most of Essex hears about it. Georgia always thinks she knows best, and Tallulah can't, or won't, be told she's wrong. Like I said, she's a carbon copy of her mother, right down to her striking blue eyes.

That's the other reason I worry. The girls turned fourteen in February, Georgia was just twenty when I first met her. In six years' time, they could potentially have men like me sniffing around them. I clench my hand into a fist and push it against my chest where it suddenly feels like I'm having a heart attack.

Lu must catch my movement, because she spins around and her hand flies to her own chest.

"Shit, Daddy. You scared the crap outta me!"

"Language, Syrup," I say in my best warning voice. That's the other thing Lu has in common with her mother, her foul mouth. She swears more than her brothers, and I blame that on her mother.

She rolls her eyes and folds her arms across her chest, and I already know what's coming.

"Don't call me Syrup."

Lu hates the nicknames I've called the twins since they were babies. She's always been Syrup, Kiki has always been Treacle.

She walks towards me, wrapping her skinny arms around my chest.

"Sorry for swearing, you made me jump. I thought you weren't coming home till later."

"I missed you all and managed to get a flight home last night." I kiss the top of Lu's head as I speak. Her hair smells of mint.

"You been nicking your mother's shampoo again?" Another cause for conflict between Georgia and Lu, they have the same taste in a lot of things. Lu likes to borrow without asking, Georgia throws a fit, and Lu tells her to take a chill pill and be flattered that at her age, her fourteen-year-old even likes her taste. That's when I generally step in to prevent my wife from throttling our daughter.

I feel her shake her head against my chest. "Nah, Mum treated me to the shampoo and conditioner while you were away. If she'd have just done that in the first place, it would've saved a lot of arguments."

I can't help but laugh at my daughter's reasoning. "I hope you also said thank you?"

"Do you think she woulda let me keep it if I hadn't? You know what Mum's like with her manners."

"Manners cost nothing and will get you a long way in life, Lu, believe me."

She doesn't reply, but I can hear her brain thinking that one through.

"What you doing up so early anyway?" I ask her.

"I didn't muck out last night. I need to get over to the stables and get it done."

"What about Kiks and Mum?"

She shrugs her shoulders and huffs. "No, they did theirs. I went to Lakeside with Harley and Jimmie. We went for pizza after. Mum said it was fine as long as I did the horse stable this morning."

She steps away from me and pours milk into her coffee cup.

"Fair enough, but take your phone." I tell her.

"Dad!" She rolls her eyes as she says my name. "You can see the stables from the back patio if you're that worried."

This is true. It had made sense to have them rebuilt reasonably close to the house. Georgia has kept a horse ever since we bought and renovated the place, and the girls have had ponies since they could walk. Kiki still rode with Georgia regularly, but Lu is starting to lose interest, preferring to spend her time at the shopping centre with her mates. I'd threatened to sell Bella, her horse, on more than one occasion, but Lu's only response was to ask if she got to keep the money, seeing as the horse *was* a Christmas present and it was only *fair*!

Lu drinks her coffee while I make one for myself and Georgia, and then she heads upstairs to change.

I step back into the office and note that apart from kicking off the throw I put over her, my wife hasn't moved. She's not a big fan of mornings and she's probably gonna have a hangover if she drank the contents of the two empty wine bottles sitting on her desk.

I park my arse on the floor next to where Georgia sleeps and sip my coffee. We have more bedrooms than the Hilton in this house and my wife chooses to sleep on her office floor.

I watch her sleep for a few more minutes. Her T-shirt has risen, and I fight the urge to run my fingers along the strip of skin showing at the small of her back.

I lose the battle, and very gently trace a line along the top of her barely-there shorts with my fingertips. She has the best arse and legs and the most amazing tits. My dick's hard again, and I close my eyes, debating whether or not I should just slip myself right inside her and fuck her and the consequences.

I open my eyes and she's looking right at me. She blinks, once, twice, and then a smile lights up *her* face and *my* entire existence. I love the fuck outta this woman.

"You're home," she states, still smiling as she speaks, her eyes sparkling with mischief. I know that look and exactly what it means, I can't help but smile back at her.

"I couldn't keep away."

"I missed you."

"I know."

"I'm so fucking horny," she tells me, whilst moving to straddle my lap.

"I know."

"How?"

"Kitten, I'm your husband, it's my job to know what my wife wants, and besides, I need to be inside you right fucking now."

I tap her arse cheek. "Get these shorts off." She stands, whips them off, and lowers herself back down onto my lap, as she does, I release my dick from where Mr Klein has been smothering him and slide right inside her.

"Fuck, T," she groans, whilst wrapping her arms around my neck. I slide my fingers into her hair and pull her face towards me. She resists.

"Morning breath."

"I don't give a fuck. Kiss me."

She does.

My dick throbs, my heart soars, and all is right in the world.

I slide my hands over her skin, up under her T-shirt, and brush my thumbs over her nipples, all while moving my hips underneath her.

"Fuck, Kitten, I've missed you."

Before she gets the chance to reply, the office door flies open.

"Dad, have you seen— What the fuck? Oh my god!" Tallulah shrieks.

"Shit!" Georgia shouts.

"Lu, language!" I shout.

There are a few seconds of silence as Lu just stands in the doorway and casts her gaze around the room. Georgia buries her face in my chest, and I wrap my arms protectively around her. Luckily, the T-shirt she's wearing is long and covers everything important. Just as I think Lu is going to step out of the room, the door is pushed further open and our two dogs, Rooney and Becks, come bounding in, closely followed by George.

Georgia screams, and I jump as Rooney sticks his nose right where I imagine her arse crack must be.

"Oh god," Georgia groans, trying to bury herself further into my chest.

"Get the fucking dog's outta here!" I shout.

"Rooney, Becks—" George's mouth snaps closed, and he stares for a few seconds, taking in Georgia's shorts lying on the floor and the fact that she's straddling my lap. "Oh my god, are you two actually having sex?" he chokes out.

"This is so gross. Who does that?" Lu is still shrieking.

Rooney barks, and Becks tries to squeeze his way between Georgia and me so he can sit in her lap.

"Get out. Get the fuck out," I bellow. "And take the dogs with you."

Lu turns to step out just as a bleary eyed Kiki appears.

"What's going on?" she asks through a yawn.

"Don't go in there, Kiks. Mum and Dad are having sex," Lu warns her.

"Ewww, gross," Kiks replies before turning and leaving with Lu close behind her.

George is still standing and staring at us. "I didn't even know you could still do it at your age," he states.

"What?" As soon as the words left my lips I wonder why I would even ask.

"Sex stuff. I thought you were too old."

I feel Georgia's shoulders shake as she laughs silently against my chest. I look into eyes the exact same shade as mine and, as calmly as I can, say to my son, "Take the dogs, George. Take the dogs and close the door on your way out."

He calls Rooney and Becks, and they trot out of the room at his side, the door closing quietly behind them.

I pull Georgia's hair gently so her face tilts up to mine.

"And what exactly has tickled your fancy, Kitten?" I ask, feigning seriousness.

"Rooney's wet nose, and it wasn't my fancy he tickled, it was my bum hole."

"Lucky dog."

"Never gonna happen, T. Besides, you're too old for that kind of thing."

"Like fuck I am. I'll show you …" My voice trails off as I notice Georgia's eyes fill with tears.

"Kitten?"

"Thank you," she whispers as tears spill onto her cheeks.

"For what, baby?"

She holds her arms out palms up and moves them around her.

"For all of this. This life, our home, the chaos, our children. Bum-sniffing dogs. For all of it. Thank you for this second chance." She smiles and sobs at the same time as more tears overfill from her pretty blue eyes. I shake my head.

"Georgia, this, our home, our kids. You never have to thank me for any of it. We built this together. Us baby, me and you. We're each other's second chance. Don't ever thank me."

I pull her in closer. My dick, which is still inside her despite the commotion that just went on around us, starts to stir, and I proceed to show my wife just how old I ain't.

CHAPTER 4

Georgia

I turn off the shower and reach for a towel, singing to Chet Faker's "The trouble with us", as I do. I wasn't a big fan of his earlier stuff, but I love this song.

I walk out of the en suite and into my bedroom as I wrap the towel around myself. Cam's lying on our bed with his back pressed against the headboard, his big arms folded across his broad chest, and his long legs stretched out in front of him, crossed at the ankles.

I know he's waiting for an explanation as to why he found me sleeping on my office floor, surrounded by empty wine bottles, and the contents of the packing crate labelled "Sean's stuff".

I know he won't ask me about it. I know he'll just wait until I'm ready to talk, and I know full well he knows I know all of this.

"That was an interesting homecoming, Kitten." He both winks and smiles as he speaks, making my insides and toes curl simultaneously.

"Well, the orgasm was unexpected but most definitely welcome. Becks' wet nose in my arse crack and our audience, *hmmmm*, not so much."

"Never before in my life have I been jealous of a dog." His eyes shine as he talks.

"Oh yeah, always wanted a cold wet nose, have you, Tiger?"

"If it gains me access to that tight little arse of yours, then fuck yeah, I can do cold and wet."

There's a moment of silence as we stare at each other. My heart hammering hard in my chest as I contemplate the conversation we need to have and the explanation I should offer.

Our relationship is based on total honesty, it always has been. Cameron King has never made me feel guilty for the thoughts, feelings, grief, or guilt I still carry for the death of my first husband.

He's jealous and possessive, but he's never ever done anything other than hold me tight and tell me to let it all out whenever I have a meltdown, which thankfully happens rarely these days.

I chew on the inside of my lip as his eyes rake over me from my head to my Racy Red shellac-coated toenails.

I try to organise my words before speaking. The last thing in the world I would ever want to do to this man is hurt him or make him feel as if he is anything less than the centre of my world.

The life we have, our children, the chaos that surrounds our hectic home life, the love we share, are all things I would sell my soul to keep. The man lying on our bed in front of me is responsible for it all, and I love him beyond any kind of measure. And yet, there's Sean. There always has been Sean, and there always will be Sean.

I lick my dry lips and draw in a breath, preparing to offer my explanation, but he shocks the shit outta me by saying, "Come over here and talk to me, baby," while patting the mattress next to him.

"Let me just put some clothes on," I request.

"I prefer you naked."

I stop in my tracks and tilt my head to the side and smile at him before starting up again and disappearing into our walk-in wardrobe. "Yeah, but we don't get much talking done when clothes don't factor into the equation and naked bodies do."

My husband's been gone for almost two weeks, so I'm more than ready to jump his bones again. First we need to talk, and then I need to organise the kids. I pull on a pair of shorts and a T-shirt, not bothering with underwear.

Instead of sitting beside him, I straddle his lap so I can look him in the eyes. Which I do, while he pulls my hair out of the messy bun I had it in for my shower and lets it fall down my back.

He pulls me towards him and drags his nose up my neck and through my hair, before tucking it behind my ears.

"Fuck, I've missed you."

"We've missed you too." I rest my forehead against his as I speak.

"So, you bought Lulah some of your shampoo? Her hair smelled just like yours when I got a cuddle off her this morning."

"Yeah, rather than keep arguing with her, I called Conner's wife, Nina, and she got me some wholesale. It meant I had to buy twelve bottles but—"

"But anything to stop the screaming matches that go on between you two?" he interrupts.

"I scream because she takes it out of the shower. I wet my hair, and then I realise it's missing. I don't mind her using my stuff, as long as she puts it back where she finds it." I let out a small huff before continuing. "We really need to have a word with her about her language, too. She's a fourteen-year-old school girl, not a twenty-five-year-old brickie on a building site."

He throws his head back and gives me one of his big Cameron King laughs.

It still does things to me, and my belly squirms.

"Oh my god, that's funny! All these years, Kitten, all these years I've picked you up about your language, and now, your complaining that our daughter sounds just like you."

"But I don't swear around the kids, you dropped the F bomb more than once this morning when you were shouting at them."

"We were shagging, they wouldn't leave the room. Then the dogs tried to join the party. Of course I bloody swore."

We're both quiet for a few seconds. I assume, that like me, he's reliving this morning's embarrassing events in his head, which I know are going to lead him back to what he really wants to know.

"I opened that old crate, the one that's labelled 'Sean's Stuff'."

"I know, I saw."

I nod my head and chew on my lip again for a few seconds.

"He would've been fifty this year, and Tom and Billy have agreed to play at the Triple M event to mark the occasion. Conner

Reed is gonna play lead, like he did the other year, and Marley is gonna front the band."

He brushes the back of his knuckles over my left cheek and lets out a long sigh.

"Why'd you need to open the box?"

"Marley's been trying to write a new song for the band to perform. I thought maybe there might be something amongst all of the stuff in there that might help him out. Marley's great with the music, but it was nearly always Sean that wrote the lyrics."

He puffs his cheeks and purses his lips, they roll together as he blows out air. He looks over my shoulder, either unable or unwilling to meet my gaze. My belly twists and turns in on itself. He's not happy about this.

"Kitten ..." he sighs out my name, and I get goose bumps across my skin. "I've always supported you. Every year, I've done whatever I can to help out with this event, and I will always do that. You've achieved great things and helped untold charities and I couldn't be more proud of you, I really couldn't." I hold my breath as I wait for the "but".

"But ..." And here it comes. "You, are my priority. When I come home early from a business trip and find you curled in the foetal position on a cold hard floor, surrounded by empty wine bottles, alone and sobbing, well, that's when I can't help but think you need to take a step back."

I close my eyes when I realise he had come home and seen me crying. I'd had my Beats on, Bluetoothing my music through them so I didn't wake the kids, and obviously missed his arrival. I feel a combination of guilt and shame as I consider how he must have felt walking in on that scene.

"I'm sorry you came home to that," I whisper, but he just shakes his head.

"Don't be sorry, I've told you a million times never to be sorry for feeling what you do, that's not the issue, Kitten, it never has been."

He rubs the tips of his fingers up and down my bare arms, once again causing goose bumps to spread down my spine to my toes, despite the fact that I suddenly feel too hot.

"The issue is with you deliberately seeking out something that you know is going to upset you so badly. That, and the fact that I'm not overly impressed with you knocking back two bottles of wine when you're here on your own with the kids."

I remain silent as I fight the urge to jump in guns blazing to defend myself. I try to remain quiet and calm when I do speak.

"I didn't drink two bottles, it was one and a bit, the first one was open and only had about a half glass worth in it. And I'm not deliberately seeking out things that are gonna upset me. I was looking for lyrics to pass on to Marley, and I decided that while I did that, I might as well go through everything that was in there. That bloody box has sat there long enough, it needs sorting through."

"Why, why now?"

"Because it's sat there taunting me for long enough. I should've done it years ago, I shouldn't have left it this long."

"Well, it's because you've always known how fucking upset it would make you." I shrug my shoulders.

"Regardless, it needs doing. It's going to upset me no matter how long I wait, so I might as well just get it done. There could be something useful in there, something that Marls can work his magic on and raise money with."

He slides one hand around the back of my neck and pulls me in for a long lazy kiss. He lets out another long sigh as he breaks away.

"All right, I understand all that. But you do it now while I'm around and not when you're here all on your own. What the fuck would the kids think if they saw you in that state?"

I nod my head in agreement. As usual, I'm wrong and he's right. "I'm sorry, I shouldn't have done it while I was here by myself. I had a few wines for courage, but they just ended up making me feel even more emotional."

"You all right now?" he asks, and for some reason, his concern touches me deeply and tears sting my eyes. He's so good to me, so unbelievably good *for* me. The emotion of the moment suddenly overwhelms me. My face crumbles as I let out a sob, wailing, "I love you," as I launch myself against his chest.

He holds me tight for a few long moments, running his big hands over my back, arms, and scalp.

"Thanks for putting up with all my shit, Cam. Don't you ever get sick of it? You must. I get sick of myself sometimes." I eventually look up at him and ask, "Don't you ever think about trading me in for someone without a shit load of issues?"

His eyes dart all over my face. "You don't have issues, babe. You just have a past. We all have one. Ours, yours and mine, is just a little more traumatic than most." He gives a small smile and then a quick peck on the lips. "That's why we work. That, and the fact that I love you. No one will ever love *you* like I do, and I'd never want *anyone* to love *me* like *you* do."

He pulls his knees up, and I lean back on them and look over his face.

"I read a few of them," he says matter-of-factly.

Shit!

"The letters?" I know what he's on about, I'm just trying to work out how I feel about that. He nods his head slowly, eyes darting all over my face, assessing my reaction.

"Are you pissed off with me?"

I'm not, not at all. I'm just not sure how I feel about it.

"Cam, shaving and leaving your whiskers everywhere, leaving the milk out of the fridge, or not putting your seat belt on before you pull away are things that piss me off. You reading those letters doesn't. It makes me feel a little bit uncomfortable though."

That's the only way I can think to explain how I feel on the subject, *uncomfortable*.

Cam has a small box of memories from his first marriage: wedding photos, birthday and Christmas cards he and Chantelle sent each other, her wedding and engagement rings. I'm a woman, so of course I've been through it. I've looked at the photos of the pair of them. She was beautiful. I know she's dead and no threat to me, but I still had to look. I'm not sure if it's a woman thing or just my warped little mind, but when I saw it in amongst his things when we first moved in together, I couldn't help myself.

"Yeah, they made me a bit uncomfortable, too," he admits.

"Then why'd you read more than one?" He shrugs his big shoulders.

"Morbid curiosity I suppose." Ah, so it's a human thing then, or is it just us two?

"Yeah, I get that. I've looked at the photos of you and Chantelle more than once." His eyebrows shot up to his hairline. Oops, I assumed he knew this.

"It's just human nature, babe. We're wired to be curious," he says after a moment.

We once again both quietly contemplate each other's admissions.

"So?" I ask.

"So?" he repeats.

"You're okay with it then? For me to keep going through this box?"

"Would there be any point in telling you no, Kitten?" I give him a big cheesy grin.

"Absolutely none, but I'll only do it while you're around, I promise."

CHAPTER 5

Georgia

I've got this thing about looking at the moon lately. It makes me feel connected to you. Because I know, with one hundred percent certainty, that during your lifetime, you've looked at that same moon. It's all I've got right now, G. The moon, the stars, and the sun. Even the air that I breathe, I take in great gulps and wonder if there's even a remote chance that it's maybe air, that at some stage, you've breathed. Is that even scientifically possible I wonder?

I know I don't bother to post these letters to you anymore, but still, I continue to write them. They help me sort shit out in my head. You could always help me sort shit out, you always gave me a different perspective, a different way of looking at things. I'm an over thinker, and I analyse everything. But you, G, just go with your gut. You react on your first instinct, all guns blazing. I hope that hasn't changed. I hope you're still the Gia that loved me so passionately. Is it loved or love? Do you think of me at all? I could ask your brothers and Jimmie but it still hurts so much G. I've tried to move on but there's nothing there, there's no connection, not like we had. It makes me panic sometimes, makes me doubt that the way I remember things is just my imagination prettying it up. Did we really love each other that intensely? We were so young, was it even possible to feel the way I think we did at such a young age?

I wish you were here to answer all of these questions. Perhaps if I had answers, it would give me some closure. It's been almost three years. Are we different people now? Has too much time passed, has too much life happened to make what we had ever work again for us? Coz I do believe that, G. It will happen. I don't know when or how, but I just know that our time will come. We will talk, we will work things out, and we will live, laugh, and love the way we used to. So, whatever tense you might be using, I'll stick with the present. I love you, Gia, and until the day you come back to me, until then, I'll keep looking at our moon and breathing in our air.

Sean and Georgia. Georgia and Sean. The way it's meant to be.

I'm sitting on the floor of my office with a cup of tea in one hand and this letter from Sean in my other. I spent all of Saturday afternoon trying to organise everything into piles. I've worked out which are songs and poems, and I've messaged my brother to come over and look through them with me. There's a pile of VCR tapes, but I've no clue what's on them; some have labels and some don't. It doesn't matter because I don't have anything to play them on anyway. There are some notebooks and diaries, a few photos, and then there are the letters.

When I had this crate shipped to me in Australia, I put what I could in sequential order according to the post office date stamps. Somehow, they got messed up, so I had to just go through them as I got to them. Because most were never posted, there weren't any date stamps, and if Sean hadn't written the date, then I tried to work it out by the things he wrote about.

I've read five letters today, but this is the first to make me cry—the first to break me. I think the thing that did it was the similarities in our thought process. I would often look at the moon and think along the same lines. Were we ever looking into the sky at the same time and thinking of each other?

Cam puts his head around my office door, which I've kept closed as I don't want the kids seeing me upset, especially over a man that's not their dad. His warm smile is gone the instant he sees the tears on my face. He comes in and closes the door behind him.

"What happened?" he asks, while squatting down in front of where I'm sitting, legs crossed, Indian style.

"Words," I reply.

He smooths some stray hair that's escaped from my messy bun and tucks it behind my ear.

"Well, words were his thing, babe. He wrote songs for a living, bloody good ones."

I sniff and nod my head. "I know. I know that ..." I trail off and blow my nose on the tissue that Cam passes to me.

It's all suddenly too overwhelming. Why the fuck am I doing this to myself? To us?

"I'm so sorry, Cam. I can't imagine how this is making you feel." He leans his back against the my pop art wall, stretches his long legs out in front of him, and then pulls me into his lap. He remains silent as he does this.

"Does it bother you? Be honest with me, does it bother you that I still cry for him after all these years?"

I turn and sit myself so I can see his face, his eyes dart all over mine and he lets out a long breath.

"Georgia, I'm only human, of course it bothers me to a certain extent, but at the same time, I'm one hundred percent certain of your love for me—"

"Good," I interrupt him.

"What we have ... Shit, I don't know how to explain this. Our relationship is unique. It probably wouldn't work for a lot of people, but it works for us, and it's worked for us for a lot of years now, baby. You were married to someone you loved deeply, that you'll always love. He died, and well, here I am. I've every confidence that you love me just as much as you loved or love him. That's just the way it is. I knew this when we got back together, and I've been fully aware of it throughout our marriage. It is what it is, Kitten. He's dead, I'm here. What's the point in me getting pissed off over your tears?"

I don't really know how to respond to his answer. He actually sounds a little bit angry.

"So is that a yes or a no?"

"For fuck's sake, Georgia, you're my wife and I love you. Of course it fucking bothers me. He's been dead for sixteen years, build a bridge and get the fuck over it. Is that what you wanna hear from me?"

I'm stunned into silence for a few seconds. Then I try to scramble to get out of his lap and away from him, but he holds me in place by my waist.

"You asked me a question; now listen to the answer." I stare at him, wide eyed and still too shocked to speak or attempt to move again.

"Part of what makes you the person you are, the woman I've loved for so long, is your passion. If you didn't still feel the way you do, or if you didn't react to his words the way you are now, then it wouldn't be you, not the version of you I love. I love you, and part of loving you is accepting that you still hurt deeply over the death of your first husband and the loss of your babies. I try not to feel jealous. I try really fucking hard, but I'm only human. So yeah, to some degree, it does bother me, but do you know what bothers me more?"

I shake my head, terrified of attempting speech in case I choke on the tears silently running down my cheeks.

"What bothers me more is seeing you so conflicted, watching you being eaten alive by the guilt you feel *because* you cry, *because* of how you feel. He was your husband, Kitten, and this is the first time you've seen these letters. Just like I'm human and feel jealous of a dead bloke, you're human and can't help but still being in love with that dead bloke. I accepted it and came to terms with it a very long time ago. You really do need to do the same, babe."

Wow.

I have no words. Everything he said is true. I've been in love with two men for around thirty years. I was in love with Sean while I was with Cam and then I got back with Sean, but either unknowingly or unwillingly, I remained in love with Cam. Sean died and just a year later, I was back with Cam, and now, here we are, over sixteen years after Sean's death and I'm still in love with both of them.

I rest my forehead on Cam's chest and sob. "But it hurts so much. It hurts that he's dead and it hurts that I'm crying for him and hurting you." I gulp in air and end up giving myself the hiccups.

"Why does it have to be so painful? I don't want him to be dead, and I don't want you to hurt. I don't wanna cry. I love him, I love you, and I love the kids. If he hadn't died, they wouldn't even exist, maybe, or would they? Would we have still happened? I don't know. I don't know how I'm supposed to feel. I'm a grown up, I'm supposed know this shit, and I don't."

He kisses the top of my head and my tear-streaked face, while holding me close. My heart and my thoughts racing.

"Oh, Georgia. My biggest worry was that you'd react like this to what you'd find in that box."

"I'm sorry, Cam. I'm so, so sorry."

I feel him stand with me still in his arms and walk through my office door. I thank Dr. Dre and his Beats for the fact that my children will hopefully remain unaware of their mother's monumental meltdown and burry my face in Cam's chest as he carries me upstairs to our bedroom.

These letters and the emotions that they've stirred up have hit me hard. So much harder than I was expecting them to.

He lies down with me on our bed and spoons in behind me. I feel drained. Mentally, physically, and emotionally wrung out, and it takes no time at all for my eyes to feel as heavy as my heart and for sleep to claim me.

CHAPTER 6

Cameron

I turn and look over my shoulder as the church quietens.

"You ready for this?" Robbie asks from beside me.

"No," I reply through gritted teeth, trying not to move my lips.

I watch as Chantelle, wearing a big white puffy dress and holding onto a frail looking Colin's arm, walks up the aisle. Her eyes are on me, and they shine. She loves me, she's in love with me, and I feel ... nothing. Not a thing.

"If you don't wanna do this, bro, then you need to pull the plug now. Put a stop to this and just both move on."

"It's too late," I whisper as an overwhelming sense of panic rises from my toes to my chest.

"It's never too late, Cam. Run. Run now. I'll make up some bullshit excuse for you."

I look my brother squarely in the eyes.

"Run, Cameron. Run now while you still can."

I turn my head, looking from my bride-to-be and her dad, who are rapidly approaching, and then to my brother, who's pointing at the doorway behind us that the vicar came through a few minutes before.

I give my brother a quick nod and move to make my escape through the small arched exit, but my legs feel like lead weights. I actually grab my left thigh in both my hands and lift it, I do the same with my right, but it's no good, not fast enough.

"I love you so much, Cameron. We're going to be so happy together." I can hear Chantelle calling from behind me.

I throw myself on the floor and attempt to crawl towards the door, but there are hands everywhere, grabbing at me.

"Come back, Cam! You promised." I hear Chantelle's voice above all of the others that are calling my name.

"Cam, baby, wake up."

I sit up, nearly headbutting Georgia as I do.

"Jesus. Shit. Fuck," I get out between gasps of air.

Georgia comes into focus, kneeling beside me and holding my right hand between both of hers. I drag the fingers of my left hand through my hair. Her eyes are wide and her mouth's slightly open as she watches.

"You all right?" she asks quietly.

"I was dreaming."

She rolls her eyes.

"I gathered that much, babe. Was it bad?"

I slide my hand from between hers and scratch my head whilst yawning. Georgia remains staring at where I just removed my hand from her hold.

Her head slowly rises, and her eyes meet mine. They're still wide, but now, they're also shining with unshed tears.

What the fuck is she getting upset for?

"Was it bad, your dream? A nightmare?"

She watches my throat as I swallow, and despite still feeling a little shaky and disoriented, my dick stirs to life when she licks her lips.

"C'mere." I gesture with my head and hold out my arms. Now, it's my turn to watch as *her* throat moves when *she* swallows. My erection not giving a shit about the inappropriateness of his appearance.

"Are you pissed off with me?" she asks quietly without making an attempt to move towards my open arms and waiting lap. Which doesn't make me in the least bit happy.

"Why the fuck am I pissed off with you, Kitten?" My voice sounds croaky from sleep. I watch as she laces her fingers together and sets them on top of her knees, rolling her thumbs around and around each other.

Georgia looks nervous. Georgia doesn't do nervous. I've no clue what could be going through that complicatedly beautiful mind of hers.

"My meltdown at lunch time. You've stayed up here all day. You've not even seen much of the kids."

I feel like I'm living in a parallel universe. I must still be foggy from sleep because I feel like I'm missing something.

"What the fuck are you talking about?" My question comes out harsher than I intend, but I'm baffled.

"You were pissed off with me earlier when I had my meltdown of Georgia proportions. You carried me up here, and we must've fallen asleep. Harry came in and woke me up because he was starving. We promised the kids TGI's tonight, remember? I woke you up, and you said you were coming, but you went back to sleep. I ended up taking them on my own."

"Wha, wait, wait, wait. What time is it?"

"Just after twelve."

"At night?"

"Yeah."

"Fuck. I'm so sorry. I don't even remember saying that I was getting up." She's still kneeling next to me, looking all wide eyed and sorry for herself.

"Come the fuck over here, Kitten. I won't tell you again." She silently slides herself into my waiting lap, and her scent is all it takes to calm my racing heart. I kiss the top of her head.

"I thought I'd finally fucked things right up this time," she says into my neck. I feel like a complete prick.

"The jetlag must've hit me and then kicked my arse. I'd never stand you and the kids up, babe. I'm surprised you would even think for a minute that I would."

I move her legs to either side of my hips and pull her in close so I can look into her face.

"You really think I'd do that?" I ask her. She shrugs her shoulders and lets out a long breath.

"I thought I'd driven you to do that." She blinks repeatedly, but it doesn't keep her tears at bay. They hang from her dark lashes, and my gut twists at the thought of her feeling shitty the whole night.

"I'm so sorry about earlier, Cam. It was so unfair of me to behave like that. You'd just come home and I laid all that shit on ya."

I don't think I can remember a time when I've seen Georgia so emotional. Opening this bloody box has had a bigger impact on her emotions than I think even she was expecting.

I've never known her to be insecure, especially about us. Not that she's ever let on to me and I'm pretty good at reading my wife.

"Baby, please don't cry. Of course I didn't stay up here on purpose. There's nothing you could say or do that would keep me away from you. Not even a meltdown of Georgia proportions."

She finally smiles and her blue eyes sparkle. She rakes her fingers through my messy bed hair, which is badly in need of a cut.

"I don't deserve you," she says while kissing my neck.

"Well, you've got me regardless. I need to shower and clean my teeth, baby. I want those little shorts and that vest gone by the time I get back. I need to taste you, and then I need to fuck you." I've already lifted her out of my lap and am headed to the bathroom like a man on a mission as I speak.

"Then will you tell me what your dream was about?" she calls out, stopping me dead in my tracks. I turn back to look at her. She's sitting in the middle of the bed with her legs crossed, looking as young as she did on the night I met her.

I love the fuck out of this woman. Have done for almost thirty years. Will do till the day I day. And if there's any way for it to be possible, I will keep on loving her after that.

"Yes, Kitten. Then I'll tell you about my dream."

We don't really ever talk about Chantelle. I don't think it's a deliberate thing, it's just the way that it is. I have a small box in my safe with a few keepsakes from our relationship in it, including our wedding rings. I haven't kept them for any sentimental reasons, I just don't really know what to do with them.

After Chantelle died, I asked her sister if she'd like her jewellery. She told me to poke it up my arse. That wasn't an option, so I put it in my safe and that's where it's stayed, mostly forgotten.

Simone Price was Chantelle's half-sister; same mum, but different dads. I've no idea who her biological father is, but Colin, Chantelle's dad, always looked after her right. Colin and I were joint owners of a club. When he died, Elle inherited her dad's share. I assumed after Elle's death, it would go to me, but she left it to her sister. I can only assume she did it because it was the only thing she had that was solely in her name. I also don't suppose for a minute she expected to die so young.

I let the heat from the jets of water penetrate my skin and sooth my muscles as I think about how ironic it was that Simone eventually sold Elle's share of the club to the Layton's. Entwining mine and Georgia's lives before we even realised it.

I would never forget the first time I noticed her walk into my wine bar. I'd spent the hot August day on the golf course, getting my arse whipped by Robbie. After, I'd gone back to my flat to shower and change, and as I came down the stairs and into the bar, I saw her.

She was tall, taller than the two girls she was with, and my eyes were drawn to her as she flicked her long dark hair over her shoulder. I moved through the bar without taking my eyes off her, desperate for a good look at her face.

I reached my brother and a couple of mates he was standing with at the bar, and he passed me a bourbon. I nodded a thank you and took my eyes from her, to meet his for a split second. When I looked over to where she was standing, she'd turned her back to me, but I positioned myself at the bar so I could watch her. I didn't have a clue what the draw was; I just needed to see that face.

I chatted mindless shit with Rob, Tony, and Gary at the bar, but all the while, I took in her long legs and the fitted black dress she was wearing. She was skinny, a lot skinnier than most birds I'd been with … well, the ones I could remember anyway. I got this weird uncomfortable feeling in my gut at that moment, like, I don't know. It just felt wrong to be thinking about other birds while I was looking at her.

My life was just getting back on track after the chaos that ensued after the death of my wife. If I were being totally honest, things had been spiralling out of control for some time before that. The drink, the coke, the women—I sampled them all to excess, and then after my marriage, the excesses became something of an addiction.

I'd married Elle out of a sense of duty and for the good of the family. Robbie was already engaged to Teresa, Josh just too young and irresponsible, and so it was left to me. I had felt the pressure to do right by the family business and marry Colin Turner's only surviving heir and strengthen the King name by tying all of his businesses to ours.

Robbie was happy, we had strength in numbers and money coming in from all over the country. We kept our noses clean and our pockets lined. We didn't step on anyone's toes and didn't encroach on anyone else's manor. We didn't need to. Life was sweet. But I was miserable. Chantelle had been around for most of my life. Our parents were friends, and so she was just there. Holidays, daytrips, family gatherings, she was there. She was pale and blonde and never wanted to join in any of our rough "boy" games when we were kids.

I didn't like or dislike her as we were growing up. I just didn't think much about her to have an opinion either way. As we got older and hormones started to play a part, things changed a little. She got boobs, so yeah, I noticed her more. She was still quiet and never wanted to sneak outside for a cigarette when we were together at parties and the grownups were drunk. She never wanted to get involved when we stuffed potatoes into the exhaust pipes of all the cars in her dad's driveway during Sunday afternoon BBQs. She would never swim in the ocean when our families went to Spain together for holidays, opting to lie back on the beach alone and watch the rest of us from a distance instead.

She was a nice enough girl, but she just had nothing about her. No spark. No sense of adventure. Nothing. And yet, I still married her.

I regret that decision every single day of my life. If I had stood my ground and said no, she'd probably still be alive today. And this guilt I feel is exactly the reason why I understand the anguish in Georgia's eyes when she cries over Sean. I totally get it.

I love my life. I love my wife and my kids and everything we've built together. I wouldn't change it for the world. Does that mean I'm glad that Elle died? If she hadn't, the life I have now wouldn't exist. I couldn't have this life without the death of another, and although I don't wear my emotions on the outside like Georgia does, the guilt is still something I struggle with on a daily basis.

I didn't love Chantelle, but I still think about her death and the death of my son every single day, so I can only imagine what Georgia goes through while battling her demons over losing Sean.

They died, we didn't. It's pointless beating ourselves up over it. It won't change anything. I love her, and she loves me. We've been blessed with four amazing children, and since I'm not a religious person, I thank modern science, the wank bank, and my sisters-in-law for that.

While I've learned to accept all of this and move on, Georgia still struggles.

Georgia.

That first night I saw her at Kings, I'd watched and I'd watched, and then finally, she turned around. She'd moved to the other side of her friend that was sitting on a stool to let someone pass, and she hadn't moved back.

She was stunning. Olive skin and the most amazing blue eyes.

The saddest eyes I'd ever seen.

I wanted to go to her and find out why she looked so sad so I could put it all right.

The two girls she was with were also both very pretty, but they had nothing on her …

"S'cuse me please, mate. Can I just squeeze in there so I can get served?" a voice asked from beside me in a strong Essex accent. When I turned my head, the blonde girl that was with Little Miss Sad Eyes was standing behind me.

"You can squeeze right in here if you wanna, sweetheart," Gary told her. She looked at the space he'd made for her and then at his hands.

"You touch my arse, and I'll knock you the fuck out, Grandad." Robbie spat his beer, Tony threw his head back and laughed, and even I smiled. Gary just stared at her open-mouthed.

"Who the fuck you calling Grandad, you cheeky little cow?"

Gary was close to forty but told everyone he was thirty-two. He was a good-looking bloke and had no trouble whatsoever pulling the birds, so why he lied, I have no clue.

"You. You gonna move and let me get served or d'ya need your Zimmer frame first?"

"I'll give you fucking Zimmer frame …"

"Gaz!" I interrupted him. "Give the lady some space," I ordered.

"What lady? There's no lady around here," he said, probably thinking he was clever.

I never even saw her hand move, but I heard the crack as her palm made contact with his cheek. I stepped between them before he could react.

Great, just what I needed. For the first time since getting out of rehab, I finally see a bird that stirs my interest, and Gaz goes and insults her mate.

"You, fuck off with the insults," I told him over my shoulder. "And you, blondie, keep your hands to yourself." She opened her mouth to speak, but I kept going. "Now, what would you like to drink? It's on me." Her mouth closed and her face softened.

"Thanks, good to see one of you has got some manners. We'll have a bottle of wine please. White, make it decent, none of that Liebfraumilch shit." That comment left me standing there with my mouth hanging open. That girl had more front than Tesco and nothing had changed in all the years I've known Ash.

I gestured to Keith, my barman, and ordered a bottle of wine and a bottle of Moët. I placed the bottle of wine in blondies hand.

"You got an ice bucket on your table?" She narrowed her eyes and looked at me.

"I might be from Essex, mate, but I've got some class. I do not drink my white wine warm."

"That's good to know," was all I could think to say. This girl was like a mini tornado blowing through.

"Take this to your table, too. I'll send someone over with some glasses and have them cork and pour it for you."

She looked from the bottle of bubbly to me before taking it. "Cheers, mate, you're a diamond," she said with a wink, sounding just like something from a Dickens' novel.

"And you, mate, are a complete tosser," she called out to Gary, who I assumed was glaring over my shoulder at her.

She headed off back to her table and her mates, while I asked Keith to go over with some champagne glasses. I ordered myself another drink and turned back around just in time to see Rob, Tony, and Gaz raise their glasses towards the girls.

I looked in the direction the boys were, and my eyes met her blue eyes, and fuck me if her stare didn't do things to my dick.

At that moment, something—I have no clue what, but something—passed between us. I knew, in that instant, I knew I had to have that girl. I had to know her, and I had to have her. Not in my bar. Not in my bed. I had to have her in my life and by my side. For good.

Oh, if only it had been that easy.

CHAPTER 7

Cameron

I walk out of our bathroom and towards our bed, where my wife is now lying naked and sleeping soundly. I watch her for a while, debating on whether to wake her, to slip inside her from behind while she sleeps, or to leave her be. Neither of us slept well Friday or Saturday night but it would seem I've managed to catch up by sleeping all of Sunday away.

Georgia's lying in her usual recovery position, on her stomach, left leg bent out to the side, both her arms crossed under her pillow. Her long hair is spread everywhere, and I take a few seconds to brush it back from her flawless face.

We argued about her getting Botox the week before I went away. She thinks she needs it. I don't. Jimmie and Ash have both had a little help over the last few years, I even paid for Ash to get a tummy tuck after she carried our twins for us, but now Georgia is feeling left out and wants to get crap pumped into her pretty face when there is absolutely no fucking need for it.

I've learned over the years that saying no to Georgia is a pointless exercise. So, rather than arguing with her and worrying that she would go off and do something drastic to herself while I was away, we cut a deal. She wouldn't have any work done until she was at least fifty, and I would grow my hair back to how it was when we first met. And as easy as that, it was all sorted. Happy days.

I pull the quilt over my wife's naked back and leave her to sleep. She'll keep till morning and my hard-on definitely isn't going anywhere.

I head downstairs in search of food. Since my body clock is shot to bits and my belly has no clue what time zone it's on, my stomach is growling loudly at me.

I hunt through the fridge for food, steering well clear of anything Georgia might have made. I love my wife to distraction but she can't cook for shit. She tries. She's spent endless hours with her mum and Marian, watching and taking notes, but nah, none of it helped.

I think Georgia just has too many things going on in her head at once. She bakes a cake and forgets if she put sugar in. She puts something in the oven and forgets that it's there. I've come home before to find the timer on the oven will be bleeping. When I ask George, "What ya cooking?" her response will be, "Nothing, why? ... Shit, I wondered what that noise was." As if the house filling with smoke and the burning smell weren't clue enough.

Fried egg sandwich, that's the only thing she doesn't mess up, but that don't help me or the kids out because she won't let us eat fried food at home.

We had a few months of misery when Marian hung up her apron, living on burnt offerings and takeaways before Georgia finally conceded and we got a new housekeeper. Her name's Christine and she comes in Monday thru Thursday. She cooks the dinner, vacuums, mops, irons, and cleans all of the bathrooms except the kid's.

The kids are in charge of their own bathrooms and have worked out their own little routine for clearing the table, loading and unloading the dishwasher, and getting in the washing if it's been hung out on the line to dry.

Our kids have grown up privileged, but we've made sure they aren't spoilt in anything other than love and attention.

I make myself a cheese and tuna toasted sandwich and open a beer. Heading into my office, I open my laptop and read through my e-mails, reply to a few, and then decide to go watch some telly.

All the time I'm doing this, I'm acutely aware that all I really want to do is go into Georgia's office and read some more of those letters.

Those fucking letters that are causing so much tension between us.

I don't care if she reads them and they make her cry ... much.

I just wish she'd hurry up and get it over with.

I just care about how upset it's making her. My telling her not to feel guilty is pointless. Nothing I say will change how she feels, so the sooner she gets them read, the sooner we can move on with our lives.

In the meantime, I just wanna have a little read through them, so if there is anything in them that's too upsetting for her, at least I'm prepared. That's what I tell myself anyway as I head out of *my* office and into my *wife's*, grabbing another beer from the fridge on my way.

I sit at her desk with just a lamp on for light. It looks like two bits of rusty metal with a bare light bulb hanging from it, "industrial" Georgia calls it, scrap metal is more like it.

The first stack of letters I come to are in envelopes but have no stamps or address written across the front. They just say "Gia" in what I now know to be Sean McCarthy's handwriting.

I open the first one, lean back in the leather chair, and take a swig of my beer.

Gia,

I'm watching you sleep as I write this. D'ya think that's creepy? I don't care if you do. I've been away from you for two whole weeks while I worked. I wanted you with me, but I understand your reasons for not wanting to go back to the States. Everyone there remembered us announcing the pregnancy on New Year's Eve, and everyone was offering me their condolences and sending you their love and best wishes. It was painful, and it was hard to hear on my own. I wanted you with me, but at the same time, I was glad you stayed home and didn't have to listen to it all.

We'll never forget Baby M. We'll always make sure he's a part of our lives. I know we don't know for sure, but I'm pretty positive he's a boy.

I can't begin to tell you how fuckin happy I am right now, you coming to the airport to surprise me and the fact you waited for me to get home before you took the pregnancy test.

Pregnancy.

Pregnant.

We're pregnant, G. We're gonna have a fuckin' baby.

My cheeks ache because I've smiled so much over the past few hours. Things will be good this time. I just know it.

We'll see the doctor Monday and make sure you get the best of care.

You can moan all you want at me, woman, but I will be waiting on you hand and foot. Hand and fucking foot. No lifting, stretching, and definitely no horse riding.

A baby, G. I'm so fucking happy (did I say that already?) and so proud of you. I'm so glad this year has turned around for us. It started off so fucked. I was so scared, G. So fucking scared I was losing you. So many thoughts were going through my head, you've no clue, babe. No fuckin clue about the dark place I was in. I was thinking all sorts. Convinced you were leaving me.

And now, here we are, out the other side, still going strong. Sean and Georgia. Georgia and Sean. The way it's meant to be, except now it's gonna be Sean and Georgia and baby Beau.

I know you're gonna shake your head when you read this, but mark my words, gorgeous wife of mine, that's another boy I've put in your belly, and we will be calling him Beau. No girls for us until she has at least two or three big brothers to look after her.

I love you. Please don't forget that. You're not just my wife and lover, you're my best friend as well, so just remember that and please don't shut me out.

I know you're gonna be nervous after what happened last time, believe me, I know. I'm fucking shitting myself, but I want you to talk to me, please? If you're worried about anything, share it with me. He's my baby too, remember? Which means I now have the both of you to worry about. That's my job, though. It's my role in all of this. You keep our little man tucked up safe and warm in your belly till he's big enough to meet us, and I'll do all the worrying for the both of us. Deal?

Right, my eyes are getting heavy. This is my fourth time zone in three days. I love ya, G. I think I'm the happiest bloke on the planet right now, but I need to sleep. Night, G. Night, Beau. Love ya both xxx

P.S. Just in case I'm wrong and you're a Lilly not a Beau, don't worry, I'm your daddy and it'll be my job to protect you till we get you some brothers x

---

My head pounds as I finish my second beer. No wonder she loved him so much. Fuck, if I were a woman, even I'd— Nah, let's not go there.

I could never compete with that. I love Georgia and my kids just as much as he loved her and their kids. I would just never be able to put it into words as eloquently as he does … did.

I don't have an artistic bone in my body. A doodle of a cock and balls is a about my limit, I might add pubes and spunk squirting out the end if I'm feeling particularly arts and craftsy, but that's where my artistic flair ends.

Georgia, on the other hand, has her own fashion line that's sold exclusively through Posh Frocks, and she's been hands on with every design. She refuses just to put her name and face to it and now draws and sketches her own ideas and is on board throughout the entire production, even modelling some of them for magazines herself.

She can sing and play guitar and she has designed a couple of custom-made pieces of furniture for our home when she couldn't find what she wanted in the shops. Even this office, she knew exactly how she wanted it to look and feel and worked with the decorators to get it to how she wanted it. No wonder she left me and went back to him.

My chest feels tight when I think about one of the worst moments of my life. So much so that I know I need something stronger than beer. I go into my office and grab my Laphroaig and a whisky tumbler.

I set them down on Georgia's desk, pour the whisky from the decanter and into the glass, and take a sip.

When Georgia left me and went back to Sean, I really never saw it coming. I honestly thought we were on the same page. We were spending a lot of our days and most of our nights together, and I really believed we were ready to move in and start to make a life together. Never in my life have I gotten something so wrong. I'd lost my wife and unborn son but nothing hurt like losing Georgia when she left me for Sean McCarthy ...

Our argument that Thursday night at dinner had been over something so petty I can't even remember what it was. I know I was in a shitty mood. I said something, she said something back, I replied, and she got up and left.

I should've followed her. Instead, I ordered another drink, sat, and drank it, thinking I was giving my angry Kitten time to calm down. I knew Benny was outside in the Jag, and I fully expected to find her sitting out there waiting for me when I finally paid the bill and stepped outside. Biggest. Mistake. Of. My. Fucking. Life.

"Where the fuck is she, Ben?" I asked him as I opened the car door and found the back seat empty.

"She stormed off up the alley, boss. The motor won't fit down there so I couldn't follow. I didn't wanna go around the block to the road in case you came out and wondered where the fuck we were."

I climbed into the front seat next to him. "Go to her place, she probably jumped in a cab and went home."

I sent Benny home and let myself into Georgia's place, using the key she had given me.

It was empty.

I was both pissed off and worried and even more angry that I cared enough to worry. I couldn't call anyone. Bailey and Lennon had threatened me with a slow painful death if I ever upset her, so I wasn't about to go there, and I had no contact details for her other brother, Marley. He'd probably just tell the other two anyway, or worse still, their dad. I most definitely didn't want Frank Layton on my case on top of everything else.

I had been having a spot of bother with a couple brothels and coffee houses we owned in Amsterdam. It was all legal and above board, but the Russians recently moved into the area and were pushing their luck. Trying to make me pay for protection. Me? I didn't fucking think so. They obviously had no clue who they were dealing with, so I sent a dozen blokes over there to introduce themselves. I thought they'd gotten the message. Then two nights ago, one of the coffee shops burnt down and three of our girls were roughed up. A point needed to be made, and it had to be made in person. We were gonna have to fly to Amsterdam sometime soon and sort this out ourselves, which was the last thing I needed. I was in the middle of negotiating the purchase of a house for myself and Georgia. I had thought it was a done deal. I had thought my offer had been accepted. Apparently, I had been wrong. I got a lot of things wrong that week.

I eventually crawled into Georgia's bed, and like the sad fuck I was, I fell asleep with my face buried in her pillow.

There was no sign of her at her flat the next morning. I went down to the shop and asked down there. I didn't know the girl who was working, but she made some calls and then told me Georgia was taking a few days off.

I went back to my flat and checked my answerphone, nothing except a message from Benny telling me I needed to get in touch with him ASAP regarding our "Russian problem". I showered and went down to my office at the back of the wine bar.

Robbie was waiting for me.

"Rob?"

"You need to fly over to Amsterdam this afternoon. The rest of the boys are on the ferry on their way over there now. I've set up a meet with you and Nikolay Kadnikov for tomorrow."

Fuck, I thought I'd at least have the weekend to smooth things over with Georgia and get this house deal done.

"Why the rush?"

"The rush, little brother, is because they slapped another one of our girls last night. Sending the boys on their own didn't work, so one of us needs to go. Josh is still in Marbella, Teresa is due to have the baby any day and needs me close, so that, sunshine, just leaves you. Flight's booked, and you need to be at City Airport by three. You fly out at four thirty."

"For fuck's sake, can't this wait till Monday?"

"No, it can't. I promised Krystal we'd get this sorted. We've always looked after our girls, and right now, they're all too terrified to take a trip to the supermarket or to pick their kids up from school in case another warning gets delivered. Krystal said Marika's nose was broken last night. These Russian's are taking the piss. I want it sorted, today. Whatever piece of fanny you've got lined up can keep till next week."

I was so pissed off by all of this, I was pacing. I didn't pace. Not until I'd met Georgia, anyway.

"Georgia is not a piece of fanny. Don't fucking talk about her like that," I warned him before sitting myself down in my office chair—the "twirling" chair.

"Georgia? Frank Layton's daughter? You still tapping that? Playing with fire there, bruv. When big bad Frank finds out, you won't just get burned, you'll get fucking cremated."

"Fuck off, Rob. He's the least of my worries."

"Oh really? Since when did your balls get so big, Bertie Big Bollocks? Coz I've never met anyone that wasn't at least a little bit scared of Frank or his psycho brother Fin, not to mention crazy fucking Bailey. You must want your brains testing."

My foot was tapping and my jaw was twitching. I was also giving myself a headache from grinding my teeth together. I wanted to knock my brother the fuck out.

"I'm buying a house, I'm gonna ask her to move in with me. We'll talk to her dad before then. Of course, whether I get his blessing or not, it's gonna happen."

"Whoa, whoa, whoa, you're buying a house but you haven't asked her to move in yet? What if she says no?"

"She won't."

"Don't you think she might wanna say in what type of house she lives in if she does say yes then? Does she not get to choose it with you?"

Fuck. I hadn't thought of that.

"It's got stables and it's near her mum, she'll love it."

"I fucking hope so, mate." He clicked the nib of the pen he was holding continuously as he spoke, something else that pissed me off. I snatched it out of his hand, snapped it in half, and threw it across the room.

My phone rang.

"Speak," I ordered.

"Cam?"

My heart bounced about inside my chest and my stomach went into free fall at the sound of her voice.

"Kitten?" I watched as my brother's eyebrows shot up to his hairline when I said her name, so I raised mine and gave him a look that said, "Not one word, dick head, not one fucking word." He picked up another pen from the pot on my desk and started clicking it. I wanted to snap off his thumb.

"Fuck. Where the fuck are you? Don't you ever do something like that to me again, you fuckin hear me? I've been worried sick. Where are you?"

I cracked my jaw to relieve some tension while I waited for her answer.

"I'm sorry. I'm fine. I should've called you last night. I didn't mean to make you worry."

Worry? Fucking worry? The three times I'd woken during the night, I'd worn holes in her bedroom carpet as I paced and tried to think where I should start to look for her.

Apparently, I did pace.

I wanted to shout at her, but I didn't want her hanging up on me.

This skinny little girl had me so twisted up in knots, I didn't know which way was up any more.

"Where are you? I'll come and get you," I said calmly. I knew she didn't have her car. It was still parked outside her flat when I'd left there that morning.

"No, no. it's fine. I don't need collecting." She sounded panicked. Warning bells sort of went off, but I chose to ignore them.

I turned the chair around and faced the wall in my office so I didn't have to look at my brother's obvious pleasure over finding out this girl had me by the balls.

"You okay? I missed you," I told her quietly. She said nothing. More alarm bells. I stamped on them till they shut the fuck up. Shoulda gone with my gut.

"I stayed at yours last night. I needed to be able to smell you. I fuckin' hated sleeping in your bed and waking up alone."

Robbie made a gaging noise from behind me. I spun the chair around, picked up the pot containing the pens, and launched it at him. My stapler followed.

She was silent. Nothing but the sound of her breathing was coming through the phone, but I could barely hear it over the sound of my own heart beating loudly in my ears.

"Georgia, you still there?"

"Yeah, yeah, I'm still here. Look, Cam, we need to talk."

No, no we do not need to talk.

"But not on the phone. I need to see you in person."

Fuck. I closed my eyes and tried not to voice the panic rising in my chest.

"Well, I just said I'd come and get you, but I only have an hour. I have a flight to catch at four thirty. I won't be back until Monday."

"Well, I'll just wait and see you Monday then."

Monday? Monday was forever away.

"I'd really like to see you now, Kitten." I spun in the chair back away from my brother, who was still rubbing his forehead where the stapler had hit him. Serves the wanker right.

"Monday's a long way off, and I want to show you how sorry I am for being such a prick last night."

"Fuck Me!" my brother whisper shouted. "I'm gonna take a piss, I can't listen to any more of this." He got up and went into my bathroom.

"I can't, Cam. You don't have to keep apologising. You shouldn't have behaved like a prick, and I shouldn't have stormed off like a diva. Go catch your flight and give me a call on Monday once you're home."

Fuck my luck and fuck those Russians. I raked my hand through my hair and let out a long sigh.

"If I could get out of it, George, I would, but something's come up with some business I have going on in Amsterdam, and I need to fly over and sort it out. I only just found out myself I had to go."

"It's okay, you go and sort out your business and we'll talk on Monday."

Tell her you love her, tell her how you feel …

"I miss you, Kitten. Have a good weekend."

Tell her for fuck's sake!

"You too, Cam. Bye."

Fucking tell her. My own voice roared in my head.

"George, I …" The door to my bathroom swung open and my brother stepped back into my office.

"Nothing, I'll see you Monday."

I flew to Amsterdam rearranged the meeting with Kadnikov and saw him Friday night. I was thoroughly fucked off with the situation and the inconvenience it had caused me. I took my fucked offness out on his face and made him see the error of his ways. It was NOT okay to hit women, and it was NOT okay to burn down buildings we owned. We would NOT be paying him for protection. He would NOT mess with us again. He got my point, along with a broken nose.

I got a flight home Saturday lunch time.

Before we took off, I called Georgia, she'd slept in and I'd woken her up. Her voice was all croaky and as sexy as fuck. I turned my back to the airport crowds and tried to readjust my hard-on as I spoke to her on the phone.

She was even less talkative than she'd been when she called me Friday morning. All I learned was that she'd gone out to an Indian restaurant with Jimmie Friday night, but she didn't drink much because she was saving herself for Ashley's party. In that split second, I decided not to tell her I was coming home and just to turn up at her place to surprise her later.

Once we landed, I went home to shower before going over to Georgia's and found a message waiting from the estate agent on my answerphone. The offer on the house I'd spent the last two weeks trying to buy had finally been accepted.

I didn't call Georgia or go to her place that afternoon, deciding to turn up at Ashley's birthday party that night and surprise her instead.

She was fucking surprised all right.

The first thing I noticed when I pulled into my reserved spot was the extra security in place, even at the back of the building. I walked around to the front, where there were not only more of my staff than usual but also faces I didn't recognise.

"What's going on?" I asked Steve, one of my head doorman.

"Private party, boss. Frank's boy, the one that's in the band? He's up there with another bloke from the band."

I looked around at the queue as he spoke and spotted a few photographers hanging about. Oh well, it'd be good publicity for the club and would most definitely raise our profile having them here.

"Who's paying for all the extra security?" I asked him.

"Nothing to do with us, boss. They came with the band. Bailey's inside, have a chat with him."

I nodded my head but I was only half listening. Georgia was inside, and after two lonely nights without her in my bed, I planned to drag her out of there just as soon as she'd let me.

I had a key with me. It wasn't the actual key to the house I'd bought, but she wouldn't know that. I was gonna put it into a glass of champagne and pass it to her.

The club was packed to capacity, and the bars were four deep with people waiting to be served. I made my way through the crowds and up the stairs to the VIP area.

Bailey stepped in front of me, blocking my path from the bar to the dance floor in the sectioned off area.

"I thought you were away till next week?" he questioned. His eyebrows were drawn down and he blinked rapidly as a look of complete panic washed over his face. It was only there for a few seconds before he composed himself. Bailey Layton looked worried, what the fuck was that all about?

"I got things sorted sooner than expected and thought I'd fly straight home to surprise your sister."

He swallowed hard and nodded his head slowly. He wasn't happy that we were together, but he'd been pretty good about things so far. I wasn't sure how he was gonna feel about Georgia moving in with me, though. Fuck, I missed her. I needed to see those pretty blue eyes that finally had some light back in them.

"Where is she?"

He shrugged his shoulders and sat himself down on a bar stool. "Not sure, but if I know Georgia, she's probably dancing. Have a drink."

He caught the attention of Kelly, one of our barmaids, and motioned with his finger between us. She brought over a bottle of bourbon and two glasses, moving the ice bucket along the bar so it was within our reach.

"So, your brother's here, the one that's in Carnage?"

"Er, yeah. Yeah he is. Both my brothers are here." He looked all around himself as he spoke. He looked like he was either in pain, or he was terrified.

What the fuck was going on?

My office door opened.

"I think George said she was gonna go to the dance floor downstairs, perhaps you'd be better off looking for her there," Bailey said, whipping the sweat that was shining on his forehead.

"Why the fuck would she go down there?"

A bloke that seemed vaguely familiar appeared over Bailey's shoulder, dangling a bunch of keys.

"Cheers, mate. We owe you big time."

I looked from the bloke, to the keys, to Bailey.

He closed his eyes and seemed to hold his breath before turning around on the stool he was sitting on. I followed his gaze.

Kitten.

"You wanna drink, baby?" the bloke, the key-dangling fucker, kissed her temple and asked.

I was torn between telling him to take his hands off my woman and smiling at her. I opened my mouth to speak when realisation of who he was started to seep into my poor, stupid, love-fucked brain.

The singer from the band.

Mac?

Maca?

Something like that.

I looked from her to him, he'd kissed her and he was holding her hand. I looked at her face. Her mouth was slightly open, as if she were about to speak, and her eyes were wide. My gaze swung back to him to find him looking at her as if she were the most beautiful, amazing creature to have ever graced the earth.

He'd kissed her.

He was holding her hand.

I couldn't fucking breathe.

"Gia, what's wrong?" he asked her gently. Love, devotion, concern, and worship all too obvious in his voice. My heart stopped beating. For a few split seconds, I thought I was going to choke on it as it crawled from my chest and lodged itself in my throat.

Two days.

I'd been gone for two fucking days.

I needed to get out of there.

I needed to … I had no clue what I needed, but it needed to make me numb.

I turned to walk away.

"Cam?"

That voice. Her voice. She was calling my name, talking to me. Hope began to infiltrate the empty spot my heart had just left vacant, and stupidly, for a few seconds, I allowed it to affect my way of thinking. I'd got it all wrong, they were friends, just her brother's band mate. She'd probably known him for years. I had nothing to worry about. She wouldn't do that to me, not my Kitten.

I swung back around, and the control I had over my own fists was hanging tenuously by a thread.

Bailey jerked in his stool. He could read me like a book. Him and I were the same, it was in our genes. We could read a person's body language from ten feet away and sniff out trouble from twenty.

Because I needed to do something—anything other than stand there, dying—I held out my hand.

"Cameron King, joint owner of the place."

"Sean McCarthy."

My world ended. I nodded my head in acknowledgment of this fact.

"You're Sean? The lead singer of Carnage. Of course." I had no clue how I managed to string that sentence together.

He looked from me to her.

"Do you need a minute to talk?"

He knew. That fucker knew about me.

I sure as shit knew about him. Sean. Her Sean.

She gave her head a slight nod in answer to his question.

I wasn't sure whose head I wanted to rip off the most—hers, his, or my own.

He said something in her ear and then turned to me, "I'm gonna go get a drink from the other bar."

Good. Fuck off and don't come back. I wanted to wrap my hands around his throat and squeeze.

"I'll leave you two to talk," Bailey stated in his rough voice.

"Cam." She reached out to touch my arm, hesitated, and then put it back down to her side.

Touch me. Please touch me and tell me that I've got this all wrong. I need that. I need you, Kitten.

"I'm so sorry. I didn't want to tell you over the phone."

No. No. No. This wasn't the way things were supposed to go.

I'd bought a house.

For us.

A fucking house with stables.

She was killing me. Every word she spoke killed me a little more.

"I thought you were away till Monday. I wanted to tell you then, face to face."

I thought she felt the same as I did. I thought what we had meant something to both of us. I flew home early. I bought a house. I bought a house with fucking stables. For her. It was all for her. I needed to make her see. I should've gone after her Thursday night. I should've told her on the phone how I felt. I should've done things differently.

"I came home early to surprise you. I wanted to see you, to tell you, to show you how sorry I am for my behaviour on Thursday night. Kitten, you remember that? Thursday. Two fucking days ago?" I was losing it.

I had never hated and loved someone so much in my life, would never have thought it was possible.

"Two nights ago, Kitten, when I stupidly thought you were in a relationship with me." I punched my fist into my own chest, but it did nothing to subdue the anger building inside me.

Georgia flinched. "I was. We was …"

I glared at her whilst battling to control the rage burning in every part of me.

I picked up my drink from the bar and downed it in one go. I needed more—more than bourbon, more than beer. There was only one thing that would give me what I needed. One thing that would make me feel like I was invincible and not dying a slow, painful, excruciating death with every word that came out of her lying, cheating, whoreish mouth.

"Sean McCarthy, now why didn't I work that one out?" I asked her through gritted teeth, barely holding back the need to throw up at the mention of his name. "I knew all about Sean. I just didn't realise it was *that* Sean."

Why didn't I? How had I never worked that one out? Because I was a love-fucked cunt that was why.

"I didn't stand a chance did I? Me or a twenty-two-year-old fucking rock god?"

"Cam, please. It's not like that. I've known him since I was eleven years old. He was my boyfriend from the age of thirteen."

She looked at the ground before looking back at me with those beautiful and oh so blue eyes.

"He's the only boy I've ever loved."

Boom. There it was, the very last of my will to live leaving my body.

"Thanks, Kitten, thanks for that."

I turned and walked away, leaving my love and my life at Georgia's feet.

78

I grabbed a couple of bottles of bourbon from the bar downstairs and took them home with me. I'd almost finished the first one by the time I'd pulled up outside the wine bar.

When I got to my flat, I went straight to my bedside chest of drawers and found an old contacts book.

All it took was one call. One call, and all of my hard work to get and stay straight the last few years went to shit. What did it matter? I had nothing to live for anyway. If I died, I died. Anything was better than thinking, than remembering her.

CHAPTER 8

Georgia

I'm not sure what wakes me, probably the turmoil that I've got going on in my head right now.

This weekend has been horrible and it is all my fault. I thought I was ready to finally have a read through all of Sean's old letters. I was wrong. It isn't just about the words they contain, it's a combination of hurt, anger, and guilt. It would've all been so different if one of us had just reached out to the other. Our lives would have taken such different paths if we hadn't remained apart for those four years.

But then what?

Where would Cam have fit in the picture if Sean and I had married and started a family at eighteen like we had planned? Would I have had him in my life? Would we have still somehow ended up together? Would our children even exist if Sean hadn't died? I always thought I would have given anything for Sean to still be alive, but I would never give up my family and what I have with Cam.

So what does that mean? What does it say about me as a person? A wife and mother?

I am so sick of it all going around in my head. I am driving myself nuts, so I've no clue how Cam must be feeling having to watch me struggle with all of this. Again.

I had never doubted us or the strength of our relationship until yesterday. When he didn't get up to take the kids to dinner with me, I really thought he'd finally had enough of me and my meltdowns. I made excuses to the kids about him being tired and forced my food down when we got to the restaurant. I smiled and joked with the kids the entire time we were out, but on the inside, I was falling apart.

On the drive home, One Direction's "History" came on the radio. I am just grateful that the car is dark and the kids are too engrossed in their phones to notice my tears.

I couldn't lose him. I wouldn't survive without his love. I went over a hundred scenarios in my head, considering different ways to convince him not to leave me.

I'd drunk a bottle of wine once I got home and the kids had gone to their rooms. When I finally plucked up the courage to go upstairs and face him, I found him still in our bed and in the middle of a nightmare.

He'd told me it was jetlag. He tried to reassure me that he was fine and that we were good, but I wasn't convinced.

I slide my leg across to Cams side of the bed to find it cold and empty. The surge of adrenalin that happens when the self-doubt I'd been suffering from makes a rapid reappearance, makes my stomach churn. I get up and go to the bathroom, before grabbing a T-shirt that Cam left hanging over the back of the chair and put it on. God, I love the way he smells. He has a half dozen different aftershaves in his bathroom cupboard, but the Givenchy he's been wearing since we first met is still my favourite.

I pad down the stairs barefoot and along the hallway to our family room.

Empty.

I make my way back down the hall to Cam's office, which is also empty. It's as I'm backing out that I notice a thin sliver of light coming from under the door to *my* office.

Fuck!

There's only one reason he would be in there, and it not so that he can add himself to the kid's growth charts pencilled on the wall.

My husband is an inherently nosey person. He, Marley, and Lennon often have conference calls about juicy bits of gossip they may have heard about someone we know. I kid you not, Ash, Jimmie, and I have nicknamed them T. M. and Z. They are as up on the gossip as my girls. For someone who doesn't "do" social media, Cam still manages to know the names of every one of those Kardashian kids.

I push at the door with my fingertips and it opens silently.

He's sitting at my desk with his back to the room, a stack of Sean's letters to the side of him, two sheets of paper in one hand, and a crystal whiskey tumbler in the other.

It's three in the morning. My husband is sitting in my office, reading the words of love, Sean, my now dead husband had written for me, whilst sipping on whiskey.

For me? Is that really the right term? He'd written them *to* me, but I'm not sure he ever planned for me to see all of them. Some, maybe. But there were a few I think he may have removed before letting me have a read.

I guess I'll never know.

Cam takes a sip of his drink and lets out a long sigh.

"What are you doing?" I ask him quietly.

The glass he has in his hand jerks in surprise at the sound of my voice, and I watch as the amber liquid sloshes from side to side. As the light from my desk lamp catches it, I can't help but to compare the colour to Sean's eyes. His were brown, with little flecks of gold, whiskey coloured. Cam's are a rich, warm brown, looking almost black when he's turned on or angry.

Tallulah is the only one of our children to get my blue eyes. The other three have dark eyes like their dad.

I wonder what colour eyes Baby M and Beau would've had?

"*Shit,* Kitten you made me jump."

And it's those kinds of thoughts that are tearing me apart. Two of my children had to die in order for the other three to exist. Is that how it works? I am not a believer in God, but surely if he did exist, he wouldn't force us to make choices like that?

"Georgia?" Cam interrupts my theological musings.

"Wha?"

"I said get your arse over here, woman."

I blink a few times before stepping fully into the room and making my way over to him.

I climb sideways into his lap. He wraps one big arm around my back and one across my hips, sliding his hand up my T-shirt so he can cup my bare arse and pull me into him.

He rubs his nose into my hair, over my ear, and down my neck. I tilt my head to the side, allowing him better access. Enjoying the sensation of goose bumps spreading across my skin from each point of contact his nose and warm breath make.

Wrapping my arms around his neck, I turn myself to face him. He's biting down on his bottom lip and his eyes are searching my face, looking sexy as fuck while he does it.

"Georgia, would you tell me if I ever weren't enough for you?"

What. The. Actual. Fuck?

I open my mouth, but he speaks again before I can.

"I know I don't get the whole music thing and your love of it. I can't paint, or draw, or design clothes and furniture. I'm not always good with words. I can't write songs for or about you like he did, but that doesn't mean I don't love you any less than he did. I just …"

My eyes fill with tears, and I don't even attempt to stop them from falling as I interrupt him.

"No. No, Cam. Please stop. Of course you're enough. You're everything. Too much sometimes."

I hold his face in both my hands and kiss him repeatedly, speaking through my tears.

"I love you, Cam. You're my whole world. You and the kids are the reason I exist. You're my everything. Every-fucking-thing. Please don't ever doubt that. These last few days, yesterday especially, have been horrible. I really thought I'd pushed you away. That you were finally sick enough of my bullshit to leave me."

"I'd never leave you, Kitten. Never, and it pisses me the fuck off that you'd think for a moment that I would."

"Well, that's how I feel about you thinking you're not enough. Why would you ever think that? You're more man than most women could ever handle."

Cameron King is the most confident—almost to the point of being arrogant—man I've ever met, and I absolutely hate that I've made him doubt himself.

He tilts his hips up and makes small circular movements, grinding his dick into my arse.

"I'm not talking about the size of my dick and the ability I have to fuck you into multiple orgasms with it."

There he is. That right there is my Cam. My TDH.

"Then what, Tiger?"

"I can't write you love songs or send you love letters telling you the way I feel."

So, that's what this is all about? I might just set a torch to those bloody letters and never read another word.

"But *he* didn't have a nine-and-a-half-inch dick." My attempt at humour fails miserably.

His face remains blank as he blinks his eyes whilst staring at me for a few seconds.

"What the fuck has that got to do with anything? My dicks bigger than most blokes."

"And most blokes can't write songs or a love letter like Sean McCarthy."

"I'm well aware of that; I'm one of them."

"But I don't need you to, Cam. That was *his* thing. That's what I had with *him,* and it's irrelevant to you and me. That's not what I have with *you*."

"No, all you get with me is a big dick and multiple orgasms."

"And four beautiful children and the confidence to know that I'm loved, worshiped, and adored every single day of my life."

"I didn't give you that yesterday. Yesterday you thought I was leaving you."

I drop my head back and stare at the ceiling in frustration. I can just make out the mural of a unicorn standing on a cloud and farting a stardust-sprinkled rainbow out of its arse that's on my ceiling.

I had it painted to remind me that life isn't always perfect. My life most certainly hasn't been and wasn't now but it was perfect for me, for us.

Sometimes in life, bad things happen just *because*. It's not "meant to be" and it's not "God's will". It just is. My life isn't about fluffy clouds, stardust, and rainbow-farting unicorns. It's about everything that's on the walls beneath the hand-painted sky above our heads. It's family photos of kisses, cuddles, and laughing smiling faces, pure happiness and joy. It's hand prints filled with our family rules and inspirational quotes, the pencil-marked walls showing the kids' heights since the day they could stand. It's love, warmth, temper tantrums, loud music, and chaos. Barking, bum-sniffing dogs, muddy football boots, and shit-covered riding boots left in the hallway. It's Harry, George, Lula, and Kiks. It's Cam and his rules and lack of technological know-how. It's me and my terrible cooking. It's everything that I thought I'd never have and everything he gave to me.

Him. Cameron King.

"That's because of my own stupid insecurities, not because of anything you did."

"If I were doing my job properly, you wouldn't have any insecurities."

I raise my eyebrows and look at him, giving him my best "You've got to be shitting me" look.

He rolls his eyes, knowing full well I have him. We both know nothing will put a stop to my insecurities. I'm a woman, they come with the job description. I give him my best smile, telling him, "You look like Lula when you do that."

"Lu's my daughter, it's her that looks like me."

"Whatever."

"Now you sound like Harry. Anyway, Lu's all you. I swear she's a combination of you and Ash. I don't think there's anything of me in there."

He looks into my eyes without saying a word for a few long moments.

"Our babies," he says very quietly.

I nod my head, unable to speak around the big knotty ball of emotion that's lodged in my throat.

"We're so fucking lucky. I've got daughters, George. You gave me girls." He says it like he's realising this for the very first time.

"Never in my life did I imagine myself with girls. Boys, yeah, I always expected boys, but never girls." I can't help but laugh at the astonishment in his voice.

"For a while, I never thought I'd have either," I confess. He holds my face in his big right hand and brushes the tears from my cheeks with his thumb.

"And here we are with four," he whispers.

"And all because of you."

He shakes his head, leans in, and kisses me oh so gently on the mouth.

"Because of us."

"And that's what you've given me. That's why you'll always be enough. When you're not busy being too much that is. You gave me *back* my life, and then you *gave* me a life. One that I could never have imagined, hoped, or dreamed of ever living."

He stands up, holding me tight in his arms. I feel safe and secure as he carries me upstairs to our bedroom. I make sure to lock the door behind us.

As soon as he lays me down on the bed, I pull my T-shirt off. Cam manages to get naked in the few seconds that it's taken me to undress.

I lean back on my elbows and watch him as he watches me from the end of our bed.

"Bend your knees and open your legs. I wanna see you," he orders.

I do as I'm told, never taking my eyes from his.

"Are you wet?" He stares between my legs as he asks.

Is he serious right now?

He's Cameron King. Of course I'm fucking wet, but I won't be telling him that. I nod my head.

"Rub your clit for me, baby. Lemme watch."

I slide my middle finger into my mouth and suck on it, hard. Pulling it out, I twirl my tongue around the tip before dragging it down my throat and through my cleavage.

"Fuck, Kitten," he whispers, taking his cock in his hand and stroking.

"Dim," Cam orders, and like most other things in this world, our voice controlled lights obey him, leaving the perfect amount of lighting for us to be able to see each other but not the room around us.

He winks at me.

And I melt.

Fuck, my husband is hot.

I watch *him* bite his lip as he watches *me* drag my finger down my belly and past my belly button, until I reach my clit.

I let out a breathy *uhh* sound as I press on the little button of nerves.

"Wider, George. Open your legs wider. I wanna see how wet you are. Slide your fingers down lower, I wanna hear your juices."

I do as he orders. The noise that action makes would leave even the hard of hearing with no doubt as to how turned I am.

"Fuck," he groans before climbing onto the bed and burying his head between my legs.

He assaults me with that big, wide tongue of his and I love it. He bites the inside of the top of first one thigh and then the other as I moan. I haven't even come yet, and I already feel boneless.

Then he pulls what we call his "master stroke" on me, scissoring his fingers, he presses his thumb onto my clit and flicks his tongue around it. His index and middle fingers slide inside where I'm wet and so desperately waiting for him and his ring and little finger sink slowly into my arse. When he works the whole lot together, I see stars.

The groan that escapes me is so much louder than I intend and I cringe in case it wakes any of the kids. Cameron chuckles.

"You like that, baby?"

"*Yes*, fuck yes."

He kisses up my belly, making me shudder as he sucks my right nipple into his mouth. My fingers rake through and grip his hair, pushing his head down into my chest harder.

He kisses a path across to my left nipple. Capturing it between his teeth, he looks up at me with soulful, dark eyes. I witness my whole world reflected back at me.

"I love you Tige—" His mouth is on mine before I even finish getting the 'r' sound out of it.

His lips are soft but so demanding, forcing my mouth to open for him. His tongue darts inside, and I gladly welcome the assault, giving back as good as I get the whole time. He rains kisses down on my face and then moves his lips to my neck and behind my ear, where he licks, sucks, and drags his teeth, making me groan and rake my nails down his back.

I tilt my hips, trying to gain friction, or better still, access to that big dick of his so I can guide it inside me.

"You want me, Kitten?"

"Yeah." Is all that I have.

"Tell me. Tell me what you want, baby."

"You, T. I want you."

"Where, baby. Where'd ya want me?"

"Inside. I want you inside me, over me, on me. I want you everywhere, Cam. Fuck me, please."

He slides inside me, joining us together. United.

He stops moving his hips and pushes himself onto his elbows so he can look at me.

"I love the fuck outta you, Kitten."

Overwhelmed by the moment, the emotions, our conversation, and admissions, I can't stop the tears that roll from my eyes and down towards my ears.

He moves his soft lips to mine, but this time, he's gentle. His tongue flicks along the seam of my mouth as he moves his hips, pushing himself deeper inside of me. It isn't enough. I dig my fingers into his tight arse cheeks and pull him, closer, harder, tighter towards me.

He's buried to the hilt, and I'm only too beautifully aware of it.

Cam does this thing. He has this way of moving that I love. He rolls his hips, pulling his dick out of me, dragging it first up and then down over my clit before burying himself back inside of me. Over and over he repeats the move. I can't even make a sound. I just lie there and take what he gives me until he switches it up and continuously grinds himself inside and against me. I move to meet his movements, and soon, I'm seeing solar systems, not just stars.

"Ahh," The only communication I am now apparently capable of.

"Fuck, baby. *Fuck,*" he whisper shouts into my ear.

The room spins. Dots dance in front of my eyes. My legs twitch as I try to back away from the orgasm that's sending tremors through my entire body. It's too much but not enough. I need to get away, but I crawl towards it, begging for more. I give up the fight and let it claim. Then I let it own me.

I can't even hold on to Cam as he comes. I feel him throb, pulse, and explode inside me, but I can't move my arms to hold him to me like I want to.

He eventually still his movements. The only sound in the room is our heavy breathing as he rests his forehead against mine.

"I love you, Kitten. Please, don't ever be in any doubt about that. Not even for a second."

He holds onto my arse cheeks and rolls over onto his back, bringing me to lie on top of him.

Without another word, we go to sleep.

CHAPTER 9

Georgia

The week that followed the best make-up sex ever had by anyone in the history of the world was a pretty good one.

The kids are busy but behaving. Now that Cam has all of his security issues sorted out at the clubs, he is happier and not on the phone as much. This means that he has time to help me with a few of the arrangements for this year's Triple M concert. The event has grown too big for his London club and now, we now hold it in a football stadium instead. KLUB still hosts the Sydney event, and Cam supplies the venue and all of the staff to us free of charge.

I really do have the best husband.

Who, coincidentally, just left this morning for a golfing weekend with my brothers, so Jimmie and Ash were coming over to stay. My twins are away on a four-day residential in the New Forest with the school and both the boys have sleepovers tonight.

I've managed to separate a pile of lyrics from all of Sean's stuff for my brother to go through when the boys got back on Sunday afternoon. Some are whole songs, some a few verses, some just a line but there could be something amongst it all that Marley can use.

I've put Sean's diaries into a separate box to look at another time. I just don't have it in me right now to read them. Maybe I never will. His letters are hard enough, the thoughts and feelings that he *wanted* me to know. I'm not sure that I'll *ever* want to know or read the ones that are private and were never meant for me or anyone else to see. His private thoughts should probably remain that, private.

On my desk sits the last pile of letters addressed to me, a pile of miscellaneous stuff that I've yet to sort through and a few video tapes, one of which I was now about to start watching.

Marian has loaned us an ancient portable television that must've been about twenty years old. It has a video player built into it and I've just pressed play when Harry knocks, then walks into the room.

He leans over my shoulder and looks at the screen, which is still just displaying white noise.

"What is *that*?"

I pause the tape. I have no clue what's on it and don't want anything inappropriate popping up and surprising me.

"It's a video clip of Carnage."

"No, I meant that, the telly. Why's it so big?"

I laugh. Harry's generation only know flat screens, curved screens, 3D, LCD and plasma. They would have no concept of the huge back part televisions used to have on them or of having to actually get up and turn it over.

"That's a little one, a portable that you would have in the bedroom or kitchen," I explain.

"Why's it blue?"

I look over the very nineties bluey silver colour of the telly.

"I've no clue. You could get them in all colours to suit your room, back in the day."

I watch him as he walks across the room to get the spare chair that's sitting in the corner. He moves exactly like his dad. Long confident strides. He pushes the front of his dark hair back before lifting the chair with ease and putting it down next to mine. He picks up a Polaroid photo that I'd found amongst everything else. It was of a hot and sweaty Sean and Marley. Their guitar straps pulled tight across their chests, their guitars resting across their backs. They each have a beer in their hands and Marley's arm is slung over Sean's shoulders. They'd obviously just finished a show somewhere.

They look so young. Twenty at the most. So it was probably at a time that we weren't together. I'd kept it out to give to Marley. I have a couple of photos of the pair of them in my office, and I even keep a photo of me and Sean in here. It was my favourite one of the two of us that was taken on my birthday. I'm around five or six months pregnant with Beau, Sean has his hand on my pregnant belly, my hand is on top of his. Both of us were looking down at our hands at the moment the image was captured.

I fail to blink back tears and swipe at them discreetly from under my eyes.

"Do you miss him?" Harry asks from beside me.

I take a deep breath while I think about how to word my answer.

Our kids are aware of the basics when it comes to the story of Sean and me.

There's lots of information, some true, some complete bullshit, out there on the internet to be found, so we've raised them with a policy of, if they ask, we won't lie, we'll give them an answer that's as age appropriate and as near to the truth as we can.

"Yeah, I miss him. He was my best friend as well as my husband. We grew up together. I'd known him since I was eleven years old."

"How did you meet, at school?" Harry asks, still looking at the photo.

"No, Marley brought him to our house. He'd just moved to our area and been recruited by the band. It was the summer holidays. Jimmie and I were hanging upside down on the monkey bars when they walked up the garden at Nan and Pops old house."

He turns his attention from the photo to my face as I talk. I wonder how much I should tell him. I wonder what's appropriate for a fifteen-year-old having a conversation like this with his mum. Are there even guidelines for a conversation like this?

"Then what?"

"Marley told me to stop flashing my knickers."

Harry laughs. "Sounds like Marls."

I won't mention that Sean asked me to show him my tits.

"And then what?"

I let out a long breath and decide to be totally honest with my son.

"I fell in love. I was eleven years old, but I knew without a shadow of a doubt that I loved him."

His brown eyes, Cam's eyes, look over my face.

"So how old was you when you met Dad?"

"Nineteen, almost twenty I think."

"But he was still alive then, Maca?"

"Yeah, we split up when I was sixteen, got back together again when I was twenty …" I trail off. Would he ask?

"But you were with Dad then?"

Of course he asks, he is Cam's son.

"We split up. Sean and I got back together, eventually got married, and were together for fifteen years before he was killed."

"And then what? You got back with Dad? I never knew that. I thought you met Dad at his club in Sydney."

I nod my head. "We met *back* up in Sydney. I was there to escape the press and the public on the first anniversary of Sean's death. I had no clue your dad owned the club. We bumped into each other and started seeing each other when we got back to England. We've been together ever since."

He picks the photo up and looks at it again.

"So, if he hadn't died, you and Dad wouldn't be together and my brother and sisters wouldn't have been born." It's a statement, not a question. I don't even attempt an answer.

"I don't wanna be glad he died, Mum, because I've seen how upset you still get about things, but I'm glad you and Dad met and got back together."

I have to wait a few seconds before I can speak, and even then, my voice wobbles.

"You don't wish things had worked out differently with your …" I can't call her his mum, she's not his mum. I am.

"Tamara?" he offers up. I love this kid so bloody much.

He tilts his head to the side and smiles at me, knowing full well I'm struggling. "With Tamara?" I continue.

He shakes his head no. "If they'd have sorted their shi— Themselves out, then where would that leave you? What about the twins and George? Without Dad, they wouldn't be who they are. They might not even exist."

He's expressing all of my own inner turmoils, and I'm kinda glad. It makes me feel like my thoughts are normal. It also makes me wonder about Cam and Chantelle. Before me, and even before Tamara, there was Chantelle, Cam's first wife.

My stomach lurches. It's as if H is reading my thoughts.

"Strange really, that Dad's first wife died, then your husband, then Tamara killed herself, and you two end up together after both going through all of that."

I nod my head, agreeing with him.

"Life's strange sometimes, mate, that's just the way it is. Sometimes it can be very wicked, too."

"And lucky. You both had bad luck, but then you had good luck when you bumped into each other in Australia. You had good luck again when Jimmie and Ash had the twins and George for you. We were all lucky Dad didn't die when Tamara shot him. That is all *good* luck and none of that is wicked."

This kid is so bloody perceptive. I reach out to ruffle his hair, but he ducks out of the way.

"What ya doing? Don't touch the hair, I'm going out in a minute."

"Where you going?"

"Westfield's with George and Ollie."

As if on cue, George comes through the door.

"Here you are. Don't you answer your messages?"

H sends me a sideways look. George's voice has broken over the past few months and is deeper than both his and Cam's right now.

I nudge Harry, silently telling him not to make fun of his brother, but George catches it.

"What?" He looks between the both of us, wiping his hand over his face, paranoid that he has something on his chin.

"Nothing," we both laugh and say at the same time.

"Does this look all right?" George asks us.

He's wearing a short-sleeved shirt, which is buttoned up to the neck, and a pair of skinny jeans that have an extra low crotch so they don't split when he tries to walk in them. Cam hates the things and is constantly telling the boys to pull their trousers up when they slide down and expose their boxers underneath.

"Yeah, you look nice. You both do."

Harry is wearing a similar outfit, except with shorts in the same style as George's jeans.

They are handsome boys, and I am noticing more and more that girl's heads turn when we are all out together.

I sort of got used to it with Sean. He was public property and it went with the job. I didn't like it, but I got used to it, to a degree. I don't like it when it happens with Cam, and it does, often. When it does, I politely explain to women in bars and restaurants that it's highly disrespectful to look at my husband like they want to ride home, on his face. But when it happens with my boys, whoa. I will glare back at the little slutetts that stare like they want to eat them with a look that says, "You're fourteen, sweetheart. Fuck off home and do some colouring, play with Barbie, put on your My Little Pony jarmies, wipe those big black scary eyebrows off your face, and go to bed."

Then Cam reminds me what I was doing at fourteen.

I tell him to shut up and mind his own business.

He laughs.

I don't.

"You got money?" I ask them.

"Yeah, Dad transferred my allowance a week early. I saw a pair of football boots I wanna get, and he said he'd go half with me," George replies.

"Dad transferred you money? How?"

"Online," they reply in unison.

"How? Dad don't know how to do online banking."

"Yeah he does. H put the app on his phone, and we showed him how to use it yesterday. His practice go was sending me my allowance."

Well, wonders would never cease. My husband is finally getting with it.

"I showed him how to send photos in a text as well. I told him he should get Facey coz it's cheaper, but he just said fu— No. He said no, he didn't need it."

Yeah, I could well imagine what Cam would have to say about getting a Facebook account. It would've been far more than no.

George looks at his phone. "Ollie's outside," he announces.

"You gonna be all right here on your own tonight?" Harry asks.

"I won't be on my own. I can call the dogs inside and Jimmie and Ash are coming over to stay. Paige might come over too if she's not too jet-lagged."

"Paige?" they both enquire at once.

"Is she bringing any of her mates?"

Like father like sons. Paige had come over for a family BBQ when she was home one time last year and she'd brought a friend. A very pretty friend. As young as my boys were, they knew what they liked, and that day, it was Kitty Calder, the young Australian model that Paige had with her. Unfortunately for them, Kitty was twenty-three and didn't even know they existed.

"Unlucky boys, she's on her own."

They shake their heads and slouch their shoulders in mock disappointment before kissing me goodbye and heading out the door.

Harry was right, I was lucky, in so many ways.

A few minutes later, I receive a text from Cam.

TIGER: Wanna see a dick pic?

ME: Depends whose dick the pic's of?

TIGER: My fuckin dick. Why, who the fuck else sends you dick pics?

I don't reply, and my phone rings thirty seconds later, and just for fun, I silence it, sending the call to my message bank.

I laugh as I think about how much trouble I'm gonna be in later.

Last night was the scariest of my life. Even now, knowing that you're safe, my hands still shake and my throat and chest still ache.

Our baby's gone, G. I only knew about him for a few short hours and then he was gone.

I'll never forgive myself for staying down at the bar, G. I should've gone up to bed with you. You're my wife, you were carrying our child, and I stayed at the bar drinking and celebrating while you was alone and in pain in our room.

I was so hungover yesterday morning, I didn't even realise how quiet and pale you were.

As soon as Jimmie mentioned it, as soon as finally paid you some attention, I knew in an instant something was wrong.

And then everything happened so fast. You were sick, and then when I held you in my arms you were so cold and clammy. You just laid there, limp like a rag doll. I can't begin to put into words the level of fear I felt during the few minutes it took us to get to the hospital.

I knew it was bad when they gave you a bed straight away. I held you, Georgia. I held you so tight in my arms, but I couldn't stop you from shaking. I didn't wanna let you go, G. I was so fucking terrified that I would never get another chance, that it would be the last time I ever got to hold your soft warm body against mine, that I didn't wanna let you go.

But then the convulsions started. George, I lost it. I fucking lost it. Marley was holding me back when they wheeled you away. Fuck George, I knew the baby was gone. There was blood all over your jeans, and I knew what that meant, and my brain was sorta accepting that. But you, George? No, I couldn't lose you. I wouldn't survive, George. I wouldn't fuckin' want to.

And then it was quite. After all the noise and chaos, they showed us to a waiting room and it was just nothing, silence.

Two hours I spent, contemplating how I was going to end my life if they didn't come back soon and tell me you were ok.

You know I'm not religious, but I begged and I prayed to anyone that was out there listening, even the devil himself. Me for you George. That's what I offered. My life for yours, but at the same time, I had to work out what I was gonna do if no one listened. I had two hours to work out exactly how things would go if you didn't make it. I'd have to make sure you had a proper funeral, George. I'd be dying inside, but

I'd get through it, knowing that soon enough, I'd be joining you too.

So, I would give you the perfect funeral, and then I would join you and our baby, George.

Then the doctor came and explained everything. Ectopic, fallopian tubes, rupture. Apparently, we were lucky, we lost our baby, but we got to the hospital in time to save you. I don't feel too lucky right now, but I'm so fucking grateful I still have you.

I love you, Gia, my beautiful girl. I love you so fucking much. This next few months are gonna be hard. We're gonna be sad, and we're probably gonna fight and cry and blame each other. We just need to remember that when it all feels like it's too hard or when it's all too much, we're Georgia and Sean. Sean and Georgia, and we're meant to fucking be.

Sleep soundly now. Tomorrow is a new day, and I will do my absolute best to make it a little brighter for you, because if your heart is as broken as mine right now, then I know just how much pain you will be feeling.

I love you, Gia, my brave and beautiful girl. I love you Baby McCarthy, I'm so sorry that we never got to meet you, but rest assured, you will be remembered with every beat of my heart. xxx

My head hurts and my face stings with the salt from my tears.

He hurt so bad after we lost baby M, and I was so selfishly wrapped up in my own grief that I never saw it. It was all about me. Never once in those first few weeks did I think about the fact that he had thought that he'd lost us both.

Aside from the anguish he conveys in this letter, I can't help but notice the irony in the similarity of the way we thought.

He planned on getting through my funeral and then killing himself if I died. When he died, I attempted exactly that.

"Oh, Sean, life was so unfair to us, babe. Can you see me now? Are you watching me? I hope you're happy for me. I hope I've made you proud."

I pull a handful of tissues out of the box I have next to me and blow my nose.

Back in the early days, after Sean died, I was convinced I could feel him around me, but that's not happened in a long time now.

Occasionally, when I'm in the car or the house by myself, I'll be thinking of him and a song will come on that reminds me of him, but other than that, nothing. I wonder if it's because he's stepped aside. That would be such a Sean thing to do, to just step away and leave me to live my life, knowing that I have Cam and the kids to take care of me.

Zara Larson's "Never Forget You" starts to play, and I laugh through my tears.

"Is that you? Are you talking to me through the songs?" I look around the room while I ask, but I get nothing. I don't know what I was expecting but I can't help but feel a little disappointed.

I throw myself down on the beanbag I've dragged in from the game room and start reading the next letter in the pile.

Why, why does it still have to hurt so bad?

When, when will it stop?
This hurt.
This ache.
I need it to go away.
I need it to never leave.
Do you feel it? This longing, the sense that something's missing.
Or are you just numb? Numb and cold.
I hope you do.
I hope we share this misery.
Just one more bond to forever tie us together.

I let out a long sigh. I feel like we had so many "If Only's" in our relationship, and as much as I regret the time we spent apart, it was all such a long time ago that having regrets over both our actions back then seems pretty pointless now.

Lukus Graham's "7 Years" filters through the sound system, serving as a little reminder of how quick life passes us by.

Three more. I'm going to read three more and then I'm gonna go shower and get ready for Jimmie and Ashley's arrival.

It's 2.48 a.m., G, and I just woke from the most beautiful dream. You were here, tucked in tight against me.

We never really had much opportunity to spend whole nights together, but when we did, it's the way we always slept. Your back pressed to my front, your head resting on the pillow, my arm tucked underneath it.

I would run my fingertips from the top of those long legs of yours, over the curve of your hip and the dip of your waist. I'd watch, fascinated as goose bumps spread across your body.

It's what I was doing when I woke from my dream, hard.

Do you ever think about us like that, G? I don't mean the sex, the closeness we shared, the intimacy? I miss it, G. I miss you. So fucking much. It's been over 3 years now since we shared a bed, since you gave yourself to me so willingly. Remember the way you used to shake, G? Whenever we used to make love, you would shake with nerves and then shake with pleasure. There'll never be anyone like you, beautiful girl. Wherever this life may take us, there will only ever be you for me. I have to keep believing that we are meant to be and one day, when the time is right and we are least expecting it, it'll happen. You'll fall back into my arms, and I'll never let you go. Until then, G, I'll hold onto dreams like tonight's, when I could smell your hair and hear your sighs and just pretend that you are mine.

It will only ever be you!

Sean and Georgia. Georgia and Sean. The way it's meant to be.

I'm done for tonight. I can't put myself through anymore of this. The girls will be here in an hour or so and I don't want them to find me a blubbering mess.

"I love you, Sean, my beautiful boy, but your words, your words just hurt my heart so bad. So I'm gonna put them away for a while. Jimmie and Ash will be here soon, and I plan on having a few wines, a takeaway, and some girl time."

Sam Smith's "Stay with Me" is playing, and I let out a long breath.

"Ok, just in case. Just in case there is the slightest chance that you're messing with my playlist, I'm gonna read one more and then I'm gonna go shower."

Today was both a good and a bad for me, Georgia. Today, we met our son. We listened to his heart beating loud and strong, and although they told us it's too early to tell, I know with 100% certainty, there's a Beau in your belly not a Lilly.

I am so happy, G, in a way that I can't even put into words, and words are usually my thing, ya know? They're sort of what I do, but I can't come up with anything that can adequately express to you the absolute love, joy, and pride I feel when I think of you carrying our son, all tucked up safe and warm in that little belly of yours.

You are, without a doubt, the most beautiful pregnant woman I have ever laid eyes on. Actually, you're the most beautiful woman I've ever laid eyes on full stop. You were pretty when you were a little girl, (I say that in a non-pervy way of course) now, though, you're simply stunning.

You take my breath away. You really do.

Leaving the hospital with your hand in mine, I felt like I was king of the world.

And then we went to lunch.

And things went to shit.

It was his fucking house, G!

Why the fuck would you NOT tell me something like that?

Why?

I know you've given me your explanation, but I've gotta tell ya, I think you're lying. I don't know why, but something in my gut just tells me I'm not getting the whole story here.

And you know what else I think, G?

Cameron King is bang in fucking love with you.

I knew it the night he turned up at the club when we first got back together, but you had eyes for only me, and to be honest G, I just felt a little bit sorry for the bloke. I knew only too well what it felt like to lose you, so I knew what he was about to go through.

After a while, I forgot that the man even existed. In all the years we've been back together, I've never doubted your love for me, not until last year when you lost the baby.

I thought I'd lost ya, G. I really thought we were done. You pushed me away time and time again until it got to the point where I almost stopped pushing back.

Almost.

And it was the thought of that poor fuck that made me not give up.

You remember that night you went out with the girls and ran into Haley White and you gave her a smack in that club Cameron King owns?

I saw one of the pictures from that night, G. It was a photo of you and of him. He was saying something into your ear and you were laughing, but it wasn't that that bothered me. It wasn't you or what you were doing. That wasn't what caught my attention. It was the way he was looking at you as you laughed.

It's the way I look at you.

I knew then that I had two choices.

I could continue to let you keep pushing me away until it got to the stage that I stopped pushing back. Until I just walked away and left you in your misery, loneliness, and depression.

Or I could fight for you and for us, for everything we had ever been through.

And you know what made me fight, G? I knew that as soon as I stepped aside, he would be there. He would be there to pick you up and put you back together, and I would be the broken-hearted one standing in the shadows and staring from the sidelines, just waiting for him to fuck up so I could be the one to step in and reclaim.

Because after today, Georgia, after watching him, look at you, at the the restaurant today, I know for a fact that Cameron King is just waiting. He's waiting for me to fuck up or for you to just up and leave me and go back to him. He's sitting tight and biding his time.

He knows there's something there between the two of you. He knows that because you let us buy and move into his house all behind my back. You gave him hope today. When he realised I didn't know shit about him owning this place, it made him think it means something, and I'll tell you what, G, so the fuck do I.

But here's the thing, I'm going nowhere. We tried being apart, and it nearly killed the both of us, so that ain't ever happening again.

So, here we are. You, me, and a baby on the way. This is our life, and that man will never play a part in it, not all the time we're together, anyway—which will be always, because I never plan on letting you go.

In saying all of that, Georgia, I want you to know something. Like I've told you many times, you're a beautiful woman. You turn heads; you always have, but I've gotta admit, he's the only man I've seen look at you in the exact same way I look at you. It's not about sex or the size of your tits, it's about you. He only sees you. And ya know what that tells me, G? He'd love and look after you in the exact way I do. So, if we don't make it, or if anything ever happens to me and we can't be together for whatever reason and he steps up, steps in and offers to pick up the pieces and put you back together, then let it be him. It'd make me happier knowing you have someone like that to look after you if I ever couldn't.

I love you, Gia, I really do. You drive me round the fucking twist. You're spoilt and selfish and so fucking inconsiderate sometimes. You're also the most *loving, caring, loyal, and compassionate woman I know. I'll take ya, whatever way I can get ya.*

I'm gonna sleep now. I just needed to get all that off my chest because it's been driving me nuts since we left the restaurant.

Good night beautiful girl x Good night baby

Beau x

I threw up.

I sobbed so hard that the sandwich I'd eaten at lunch time came up.

That letter, that information was as hard to digest as that sandwich had obviously been.

I splash my face with water in the downstairs bathroom, rinse out my mouth, and then head to the kitchen to pour myself a large glass of wine.

I'm shaking from my head to my toes. Even my insides shake.

All of these years, all of the guilt. If I'd have only gone through that box when I was in Australia.

What if I had, though? If I'd known I had Sean's blessing, would I have gone out of my way to seek out Cam? Would that knowledge have changed the course of our relationship if I'd gone chasing after him?

I gulp down the glass of wine and pour myself another before going up to my bathroom to take a shower. I put my music on and stand under the jets of hot water as "I Can't Feel My Face" by The Weeknd blasts out of the speaker above my head. The best thing about being home alone is being able to play my music loud without anyone moaning at me.

The kids like my music, mostly, although George had a strong aversion to The Jam, which makes me feel like I have failed as a mother in some small way, but he is, at least, a huge fan of The Clash, so I got something right with him.

For teenage girls, the twins have pretty good taste, they hadn't been into Bieber until he brought out his *Purpose* album, which even I agree is pretty good. They like certain songs by 1D, but not everything. They love Ed Sheeran, The Weeknd, Chet Faker, and Ellie Goulding. Nothing that would make my ears bleed too badly. Harry loves his rap. Eminem, Kendrick Lamar, Skepta, and Devlin are all on repeat on his playlist.

I am trying to focus on anything other than the words Sean wrote in the last letter I read. I feel like an enormous weight should've been lifted from my shoulders, but so far, I don't. I don't know how to let it go. The guilt has been around for so long that it has become embedded in my psyche, in my bones, part of my DNA.

An old song by the New Radicals comes on, and I sing "You Get What You Give" at the top of my lungs. It's a feel good sort of song, and I smile as I belt it out.

Imagine Dragons' "Demons" starts to play. I sob so hard that my legs stop working. I curl into the corner of our shower and cry until, once again, I start to heave.

That's where Jimmie finds me twenty minutes later.

Without saying a word, she turns off the water, wraps me in a towel, and helps me stand. We walk out to my bedroom, where she sits me on the edge of the bed.

Thirty Seconds to Mars's "Do or Die" is making the walls of my house shake.

Jimmie finds the remote to the sound system and turns it off.

"What the fuck happened, George?" she asks from where she's now kneeling in front of me.

I point my finger to the ceiling and can't help laughing when she says, "A song? A fucking song did this to ya?"

I smile up at her, tears still spilling down my cheeks.

"I love you," I tell her.

"You pissed?" she asks, wearing a frown.

I shake my head. "I love that you knew that I meant music when all I did was point my finger to the ceiling."

She smiles back.

"What the fuck happened?"

"Lemme get dressed, and I'll show you."

She stands and walks towards the door.

"I'll go and pour us a wine. Ash should be here soon. Paige said she'll be over once she showered and got herself together."

"How is she?" I ask.

Paige has been modelling in South America for the last two months. While she was there, she got so sick that Jim had to fly over to be with her for a few weeks. She'd apparently recovered enough to finish the shoot but has flown home to stay with Jimmie and Len for a while.

"Too skinny and absolutely exhausted. Apparently, she has news but doesn't wanna talk until she's fully awake."

She heads downstairs while I attempt to get my shit together.

CHAPTER 10

Georgia

We've piled three beanbags in a circle on my office floor and are sprawled out on them. The pile of letters I've already gone through is sitting in the middle, and I have the last few I haven't yet read in my lap. Jimmie, Ash, and I drink wine as we make our way through Sean's words.

There's been tears and a few "Oh George," comments as they've read, and moments where we've each read lines aloud to each other. Sean was in Jimmie's life for even longer than he was in mine. She got him for the four years we were apart, and his death hit her hard. My subsequent suicide attempts led to Jim seeking help for the depression she was in, and she'd spent a few years on antidepressant and antianxiety medication. She'd sought the help she needed and was in a good place nowadays.

I have no secrets from these two, except one, everything else about my life they're aware of and I have no issue with them reading the letters. The only one I haven't shown them yet is the one that caused my melt down earlier.

A lot of the letters Sean's written are just notes really. Words that are short and simple.

I watched the sunrise over a lake in Italy this morning. I wish you were here to see it with me. One day, G, one day I'll bring you back here with me and we'll experience this together. I love, and I miss you.

Sean x

He kept his promise. We made a few trips to Lake Como over the years, and we always woke early and watched the sunrise when we were there.

I'm in the back of a big stretch limo. It's six in the evening and the streets of Paris are gridlocked. Our hotel is only supposed to be a half-hour drive from the airport, but we spent an hour signing autographs and posing for pictures before we could even leave, and now we've been sitting here in traffic for an hour, barely moving. I'm so over it, G. I'm sick of the travelling. I wish you'd change your mind and fly out here and meet me. I understand you don't like this city, but shit, babe, it was five years ago. We're together, all of that shit's behind us. I'll call you when, or if, we ever make it to the hotel. I miss you. I'm thinking of you. I just wanted you to know.

Love ya, G.

Sean

X

I tilt my head up and stare at my cloud-covered ceiling, trying to remember when he could've written this. I rarely went to Paris with him. I know it's pretty, but for me, it most definitely was *not* the city of love. For me, it was the city of Whorely.

I'd found a photo earlier, it is of no one in particular, just a wide-angled lens shot of what is obviously back stage somewhere. I'd spotted the back of Sean's head and a side view of Marley, but the face that had jumped out at me was that of Rocco Taylor. The man who had set out to ruin my life. I'd ripped the photo into tiny pieces and thrown in the bin. Then just for good measure, I'd emptied it into the sink and set light to each and every piece.

I knew he couldn't hurt me. The evil bastard has been dead for a few years now. Accidental drug overdose all alone in a hotel room. Shame it couldn't have been something much more painful, but still, dead was dead right?

I shuddered, and just for a few seconds, I felt guilty for thinking ill of the dead.

Then I spat on the ashes that remained in the sink.

"Fucker," was only word I could think of saying as I wiped my chin.

"Unbreak My Heart" by Toni Braxton is playing over my office sound system, and I have to smile at the way every song on my playlist—no matter the era or genre seems to be relevant to my life, whether this is divine intervention or pure coincidence, I have no clue.

"Did you talk to Cam about getting a bit of tox in your chops?" Ashley asks me, while sliding across my beanbag and putting her head in my lap.

I move the pile of letters that had been sitting there before answering.

"I did."

"Blatant no?" Ash asks as I stare down at her.

"Not a blatant no. He asked me to wait until I'm fifty."

"What, why?" Jimmie looks up from the letter she is reading.

I shrug my shoulders. "He reckons I don't need it yet. He's worried it'll change the way I look and I won't be happy with the results."

"But just a little preventative won't hurt. He won't even notice." This from Ash.

"I'm not fussed; I can wait until I'm fifty. It's no biggie. Anyway, we've done a deal."

Ash smiles up at me and wiggles her eyebrows. "Oh yeah, what kind of deal?"

"You finally gonna let him have anal if you can have Botox, G," Jimmie asks with a grin all over her face.

"No. I'm bloody will not. Ladies, his King Dick has ruined my Mildred. I'm not letting it ruin my arse as well."

"Oh, come on, George, you've never even squeezed …" Ash trails off, but I've already worked out what she was about to say.

"No, I haven't ever squeezed babies out my vag, Ash, but I have had six-foot-five, and two hundred thirty pounds of pure male pounding a nine and a half inch dick into me for quite some time now, so no, my mildred is not as tight as it used to be, and no, that will not be happening to my arse. Can you imagine? It'd end up all lose and I'd be farting every time I bend over."

"*Meeehhh*, what's a few arse farts between husband and wife? It's the fanny farts that crack Marley up."

I spit my wine, barely missing Ashley's face.

"Oh my god, Ash. It's happened to me before, I just about died," I admit. Glowing crimson at the memory.

"What, you varted? Was it during sex?"

This time I choke on my wine. I have tears rolling down my cheeks caused by both coughing and laughing.

It feels so good to laugh.

I nod my head, because I'm struggling to talk.

"We were in Fuerteventura on holiday and it was hot and sweaty, and I was just really wet. I was mortified, but Cam just laughed."

"What's there to be embarrassed about? It's only air, and it's their fault any way for pumping it into ya. Marley just laughs and says, 'What's your next trick' or 'I'll name that tune in three'."

"I don't have that problem anymore. Got it all taken care of."

Ash and I share a look and try to straighten our faces before Ash sits upright and we both look at Jim.

"Wha'd'ya mean, 'you've had it taken care of'?" Ash asks before I can.

Jimmie shrugs her shoulders.

"That little cruise Len and I took in February? We didn't go on a cruise. We went over to the States, and I had a bit of reconstruction done."

"On your Mildred? Why?" I ask in disbelief.

"Why the fuck didn't you tell us? I would've come and had it done with ya." Ash sounds genuinely put out.

"Did it hurt?" we both ask at the same time.

"Why? Because my poor little vag has had to squeeze out four Layton and one King head. Five babies, ladies. Those kind of numbers don't leave things looking too pretty down there. I didn't tell ya coz, well, you know. It's a bit embarrassing. It's all right you girls knowing but I didn't want Cam and Marley knowing that I had a baggy fanny and could vart the national anthem."

Ash and I get the giggles again. I lean forward and pull the wine from the ice bucket sitting on the floor between us. I share the last of its contents around.

"And I wouldn't say it hurt. It was just uncomfortable for a few weeks until the stitches dissolved."

"Was it worth it?" I ask, genuinely interested.

"Absolutely," Jim replies without hesitation. "I now have a designer vagina. The Gucci of Coochies."

"The Versace of Vagies," Ash adds.

"The Louboutin of Labia," I gasp out. Fighting for breath as we all laugh hysterically.

"The Prada of Pussies," Jimmie cackles.

"The Burberry of Beavers," I add.

"It comes with a matching brolly and a trench coat for when things get too wet." I worry that Jimmie is gonna throw up as she laughs and talks at the same time.

"The Mimco of Minges."

"The Vuitton of Vulva."

"No, gag, hate that word," I gasp out at Ashley's last suggestion.

"What, Mimco?" she asks.

The noises we're making don't even sound human as we laugh and gasp for breath. I snort, which makes the other two laugh harder.

"The Saint Laurent of Snatches." I don't even know who says that last one, the voice sounds so strangled and I'm blinded by tears.

"The Cavalli of Cunts." I just know that's Ash.

We all lie back and gasp for air, the giggles and laughter still randomly breaking out.

"Oh my days, I needed that laugh," I say to no one in particular.

I sit up straight, forcing Ash to get her head out of my lap, where she's once again resting it, and take a sip of my wine.

"So come on, spill, Georgia Rae. What the fuck was going on when I got here earlier?"

I knew Jimmie wouldn't let it drop. What I don't know is how she managed to fill Ash in on my "moment" already.

"Yeah, what's going on, Slutster? I've revealed my varting abilities, Jim's revealed all about her designer vagina, now you need to spill the deets about your meltdown. What the fuck happened?"

Jimmie stands up. "Hang on, we need more wine for this." She heads off to the fridge while I retrieve the letter from my desk.

Once we're topped up and I've settled the girls side by side so they can read at the same time, I pass them the two sheets of paper.

They each take a sip of their wine and start to read.

Ashley looks up at me a couple of times. Jimmie's hand goes to her mouth, drops, and then goes back a total of three times.

"Wow," Jimmie states as she finishes.

"*Fuck*!" Is all Ash has to offer.

We all look at each other, shaking our heads.

"It's like, I dunno. It's almost like he had a premonition, but at the same time, he seemed convinced he wasn't going anywhere," Jimmie says.

"Yeah, but this is Sean. He'd do anything to protect and not worry me. If he had a feeling that something was gonna happen, he'd never have let me know."

"How'd you feel, George, after reading that, how'd ya feel?"

I move from where I was leaning against my desk and sit back down next to the girls.

"I really don't know, Jim. I had that crate shipped to Australia, but the time wasn't right, so I just packed it all up and shipped it back without reading them, well except one I think."

We're all quiet for a few long moments. Jimmie and Ash obviously trying to digest Sean's words the same way I had ...*was* still trying to in fact.

"George, if I ask you something, will you be totally honest with me."

My mouth fills with saliva, the way it does if I'm about to vomit, as I nod my head at Jim's question.

"Of course, go for it."

Jim stands and takes up the spot I was in earlier and leans her arse against my desk.

Ashley puts her head back in my lap and takes a hold of the hand not containing my wine glass.

"Did anything ever go on between you and Cam, once you were back with Mac?"

Despite having to swallow hard to get rid of the excess fluid in my mouth, it now feels incredibly dry. I take a long draw from my glass, look down at Ash, and then across to Jim.

I know I can tell these girls anything. They've loved and supported me through the worst of times and celebrated with me during the best. And they have never ever judged. This is the only thing I have ever kept secret from them. Admitting to myself what happened between me and Cam is harder than saying it out loud.

I nod my head slowly, and a very lost and lonely, stray tear makes its way down my cheek.

Ash pulls her hand from mine and reaches up and brushes it away.

"Don't cry, George, it was all a very long time ago. You don't have to tell us if you don't wanna."

I let out a loud sob. Despite the release, my jaw trembles when I try to speak.

"It was the night I kicked the shit out of Haley White."

Jimmies eyebrows raise up towards her hairline. Her eyes dart around the room, and I can almost hear her brain tick as she recalls that night.

"What? When? We all stayed at the loft that night, you came home with us."

"His office," Ash says from my lap.

"We left, he asked you to stay. You fucked him in his office."

I nod my head slowly. "That's exactly what happened."

"Fucking hell, George." Jimmie says before finishing the contents of her wine glass.

"It was just that one time. We never did it again, not even in Australia when we spent the night in the hotel room."

I was suddenly too hot and felt shaky.

"Fuck, I thought you and Maca had an epic love story, but you and Cam, that's just … I don't even know what to say, George. You're like, magnets or something. Parts of a puzzle that just have to be together," Ashley whispers quietly.

"And Maca's letter just makes it all even more … I dunno. What's the right word? Surreal?" Jimmie asks.

I press my fingertips into my forehead and squeeze my eyes shut for a few seconds.

"I've no clue. I'm at a loss for words really."

"Me too," says Ash, still whispering for some reason.

I pull my head back, draw in my eyebrows, and say at the exact same time as Jim, "Bullshit."

We all laugh and it breaks the tension a little bit.

"Please don't ever tell Marley," I tell Ash, now being totally serious. She shakes her head.

"Hoes Code, babe. I won't breathe a word."

I lean forward and kiss her forehead.

"So, after all these revelations, did you find anything that Marley might be able to use?" Jimmie asks. "What are these?" She picks up the pile that I'd mentally labelled "miscellaneous".

"I don't know. I set all of the song lyrics and poems over there for Marls to go through, but that was just a pile of stuff that ..." I shrug my shoulders, "I don't know what they are, so I just set them aside."

Jimmie has a white envelope in her hand. Whatever's inside is quite bulky as the envelope looks like it's full.

"Can I?" Jim asks.

"Go for it."

She sets to opening the envelope carefully.

"Over the desk or against the wall?" Ash asks quietly.

"Why the fuck d'ya keep whispering? There's no one else here."

She turns her head to look at Jim, who's now reading intently.

"I know but it's just so..." She wriggles her little body. "Sexy and sordid."

"Cheers," I tell her. "And FYI, it was neither. Not, I don't mean it wasn't sexy and sordid, because it was both of those things. What I mean is, I tried to leave, he slammed the door shut, spun me around, and fucked me against the door."

"Squeeeeeeeee! It's like a scene from a book or a film. Fuck, I can just imagine TDH being all alpha and domineering."

"Oh."

I look up at Jimmie.

"What?"

Ash asks before I can.

I don't miss the look Jimmie shoots her, and my stomach does a little forward roll, dragging the rest of my internal organs with it.

My eyes scan over what she's reading. There's a couple of sheets of paper in one hand and an envelope in the other.

I can't see who it's addressed to, but I can see that it's not Sean's writing on the envelope.

"Can I see that please?" In my head I ask calmly, but in reality, I just know my voice shakes.

I don't know why I feel the panic rise from my toes to my chest. Instinct? Some kind of sixth sense? I have no clue, but I'm anxious to the point where I feel sick. My mouth's dry, and I watch my hand shake as I hold it out for the letter that Jimmie is reading.

"George, I don't think ..."

"Pass me the letter please, Jim."Absolut

I feel the weight of Ashley's head lift as she sits up, but I keep my eyes on Jimmie. Hers dart to Ash and then back to me. Resignation written all over her face.

I know what's coming even before she says the word.

"No."

I nod my head slowly. My heart pumping the blood around my body so hard that a vein in the side of my neck actually aches from the pressure.

"Give me the fucking letter, Jim."

"George, if she—"

"Ash, I love you dearly, but stay out of this, babe."

I stand and take the two steps to where Jimmie leans back against my desk.

I don't ask this time, I just slide the two sheets of paper from between her fingers and start to read.

After the first few lines, the words stop making sense. The letters dance around the page, and my head begins to spin.

I close my eyes for a few seconds and wait for the world to right itself. All the while knowing, that after what I'd just read, my world will never really be right again.

Sean,

Please, please read this. You won't take my calls, and we really need to talk.

I can't believe you're going back to her. You told me it was over. You made me fall in love with you all over again. You gave me hope that finally, finally you would choose me, but just like last time, you've gone back to her. Why? Why her and not me? Is it because she lost the baby? Are you just feeling sorry for her, is that it? You can't base a marriage on pity, Sean. It should be based on love, trust, and understanding, and you two don't seem to have any of that for each other. She's pushed you away for nearly three months, and I haven't seen you doing much to stop her. She lost a baby. It happens all the time. What about me? What about our baby? You didn't care about me or that I was left all on my own to make the worst choice a woman ever has to make. Just think, if you hadn't left me and gone back to her all those years ago, we would have a ten-year-old now. A brown-eyed boy or girl that looked just like you. I suppose its Karma, really. I was forced to give up our child because you left me for her, so I suppose it's only fair that she loses her baby too. Funny how life works out.

I'd like to say that I wish you both well, but I don't. You used me ten years ago, and I stupidly let you use me again. I thought this time was different. I was there for you, holding you tight, wiping away your tears, and making you feel better, wanted, loved. Me. Not her.

I'll give you a week, Sean. A week to see sense and come back to me. A week to see that she's nothing but a spoilt, selfish, heartless princess who doesn't care about anyone other than herself. If you don't get in touch within the week, then please don't ever get in touch with me again. Don't contact me. When we work together, just pretend I don't exist, because for all intents and purposes, you'll be dead to me.

Carla

I surprise myself with how calm I remain. My heart's galloping in my chest and my jaw feels so rigid, I struggle to speak.

I pass the letter to Ash with a shaking hand and look to Jim. "Who is she?"

Jimmie licks her lips before answering. "She worked with the producers. She was one of the sound engineers. They had a thing going on for a while, right before you two got back together. I had no clue about anything after that or about a baby."

I let out a long breath. "You never knew?"

Jimmie looks like I've just kicked her puppy. "Georgia, you're seriously asking me that?"

I feel like the biggest bitch.

"No, I'm sorry. I shouldn't have even asked that."

"I'll tell you what I do know, though, and you are not gonna believe this …"

I raise my eyebrows and shrug, urging her to go on.

"That night you got busy with Cam in his office, something went on between Maca and her at that football match they performed at in France."

"Oh my god, yes. I remember hearing something about that too," Ash pipes up from beside me.

"What the fuck ladies? And neither of you thought to tell me?"

Ashley shakes her head, and the rapid movement is making my head spin again. "It was nothing bad, George. From what I remember, she made a pass at Maca, Maca told her to fuck off, and then he changed their flights. That's why the boys came home early. It was months later that I heard about it, and you two were all loved up and pregnant again by then. It was trivial, a couple of the girls from the label gossiping when I was there waiting for Marley to get out of a meeting one afternoon. I think she was there at the meeting and that was why the two office girls were chatting about it."

I stand and hold out my empty wine glass to Jim, and she tops it up.

I want to throw the glass, as well as the bottle, against the wall. I want to punch something. I want to cry, but I'm not sure why. I don't even know for sure what, or even if, he did wrong.

"That's pretty much what I heard," Jimmie's voice brings me back to the conversation going on around me. "And like Ash said, by the time I heard anything, you were pregnant. It was a non-story. Plus, I know what you're like. I didn't want you getting upset about it or turning up at the studio, ready to knock seven kinds of shit out of the girl."

"Girl? How old is she then? Is she young?"

My paranoia is getting the better of me. It'd always been my biggest fear when I was with Sean. He was surrounded by so many women. So much very willing temptation surrounding him. Younger, slimmer, prettier.

"George, get a grip, will ya? No, she's not a girl; she's about the same age as us. He wasn't interested, George, she was a distraction. I remember talking to him about her the first time around. She meant nothing to him. The second he was back with you, it was over."

"He got her pregnant."

"Yes, by the sounds of it he did, but she got rid of it from what I just read."

My heart broke more at that news, than at the thought of Sean cheating on me. He could've had a child. Then there would've at least been something left of him.

"What about the second time? When I lost the baby? He said in that other letter that he came for me because he knew if he didn't that Cam would. Is that even true? What happened between them? Was he sleeping with her while I stayed at my mum's?"

"I don't know. I honestly don't know, George."

I let out a long breath and sit myself back down in a beanbag.

"Holy fucking fuck. Who would've thought, all these revelations were sitting in this ol' box." Ashley lets out a long whistle as she finishes speaking.

"I have no clue what to make of all this. I've put him on such a pedestal for all these years. He was the loyal, faithful husband, while I was the cheating whore of a wife, but he was just as guilty as I was. Then, to top it all off, he tells me to be with Cam. I mean, what the fuck? What do I do with all this? Everything I thought was us, me and Sean, really wasn't." I start to cry. I fight it and fight it, but I lose, and I'm so fucking angry with myself for crying that it makes me cry more.

"I've felt so much guilt. I convinced myself that I lost Baby M because I fucked Cam. All these years, I've felt so much guilt over what Cam and I did, for moving on so soon, and for going back to Cam. It was all pointless."

Ashley jumps up from beside me and stands with her hands on her hips.

"Right, stop your snivelling just for five fucking minutes and listen up."

I shoot a look across to Jim, who just frowns and shrugs her shoulders.

"You and Sean were not a fucking fairy tale couple. You were real people, with real problems. No marriage is perfect, not a single one. I don't know why, for all these years, you've thought that yours and Sean's was, but it wasn't. So, build a fucking bridge and get over it. You were two people who loved each other passionately. No one will ever call that into question, but that alone does not make for a perfect marriage. Sadly, Sean died. Sean died and you lost Beau and it was horrible, fucking awful, George. Not just for you either, I might add, it was fucking horrible for all of us. Then you got lucky. You got so *fucking* lucky. TDH did exactly what Sean predicted he would. He swept in, he picked you up, and bit by bit, he put you back together."

She pauses to take a swig of her wine, and I take that moment to draw breath. Apparently, while she was speaking, I'd forgotten to breathe.

"Where you go from here is entirely up to you. You either finally accept that what you had with Maca was beautiful, but far from perfect, and move on, enjoying the amazing and wonderful life you have with Cam and the kids guilt free. Or you ignore everything that you've discovered by reading these letters and continue living half a life, weighed down with the unnecessary guilt you feel because of past actions that can never be changed. What's it gonna be? You finally gonna give Cam everything, every little piece that makes you who you, or are you gonna keep riding the 'I'm Not Worthy' train?"

The three of us sit in silence.

"I Will Survive" by Gloria Gaynor starts to play and totally in sync, the three of us look up towards the speakers in the ceiling. We start to laugh. I wipe the tears from under my eyes.

"It's time," I say quietly.

"Yes, it fucking is," Ash states before high fiving me.

We put the letters away and have a party for three in my office. We set my "Old Skool Club Classics" playlist up and dance the night away. The last thing I remember is singing Alison Limerick's "Where

Love Lives" into an empty wine bottle. All of us finally crashing in my bed at around four in the morning.

Despite the lateness of the hour and the wine I've consumed, I can't sleep. I toss and turn for about half an hour before Ash whisper shouts, "Stop fucking thinking, George. The sound of your brain is keeping me awake."

"I can't help it."

"Yes, you can," Jimmie joins in. "Like Ash says, build a bridge and get the fuck over it. You are both the unluckiest and luckiest person I've ever known. It's about time you started enjoying the good and letting go of the bad. Life is short and then you die. You know first-hand how that one works. Time to move on, George. We're all sick of ya whining."

"Yeah, bored. Bored. Bored," Ash adds.

"Gee, thanks ladies."

"Anytime. Now, go to fucking sleep before I put this pillow over your head."

"And I help her hold it down," Jimmie offers.

I go to sleep.

EPILOGUE

I put the potato salad I just made into the fridge. I've followed Marian's recipe to the letter and can only hope and pray I haven't fucked it up. There was very little cooking involved, except for parboiling some potatoes and frying the bacon, so I have every hope.

I know he's there before I even straighten up. The hairs on the back of my neck stand on end as his big arms slide around my waist.

He trails kisses over my neck before whispering in my ear, "I'm gonna slap that skinny little arse of yours till it's raw next time you ignore my texts and calls. Whose dick indeed." He bites and then sucks my neck. "I've missed you so fucking much, Mrs King."

I turn myself around in his arms and wrap mine around his neck. "You have no idea, baby. No fucking idea."

He claims my mouth, and it takes me less than a second to surrender.

I waited for Dido to start playing "White Flag". But instead, it is Shine Down's "Second Chance" that comes over the hidden speakers.

"Get a room you two. Where are the beers, big man?"

I look around Cam's broad chest to see my brother trying to get around us to the fridge.

"Big brother Marley, me and you need to talk."

He stops in his tracks. "We do? About what?"

I'm not gonna hold back, I don't care that Cam is here to witness this. I don't want there to be any secrets between us, and I want the truth from my brother. What's done is done, nothing can be changed now, and I'd just like to know the truth. He either slept with her while we were together, or he didn't. Whatever the answer, I'll live with it. It'll hurt and I'll be pissed off. I am, in fact, pissed off but I'm not as angry as I should be. I don't know if that's because of my age or because I've got my head around the idea that neither of us were perfect. If Marley doesn't know the truth, well then I'll just have to live with that, too.

"Carla."

Not missing a beat or breaking eye contact with me, Marley nods his head slightly.

Cam steps to my side with one arm still around my waist, holding me against his side.

"Honest to god, George, there's really not much to tell. They were together on and off when you two were apart. They were never exclusive, and I don't think she was anything more than a warm and willing body. Apparently, she got pregnant, but because he got back together with you, she terminated the pregnancy without even letting him know. She announced it in a room full of people years later, and he distanced himself from her completely after that." I watch his throat move as he swallows hard.

"When you lost the baby on New Year's and things were a little rough between the two of you, she started sniffing around. He wanted no part of it, George. Despite the fact that you kept pushing him away, despite the fact that he was grieving for the loss of his baby just like you were, he kept her at arm's length. She turned up at your house in Hampstead and made a pass at him. I walked in."

Whoa. He knew? Marley knew and never said anything to me. The disappointment I felt at that moment almost floored me.

"Don't look at me like that, George. I walked in on him pushing her away. Things weren't good between the two of you as it was, and I wasn't about to make them worse. He told her to leave. He went to Mum's the next day and you two sorted your shit out, and that was it."

I nod my head, hating the fact that I actually understand why he didn't say anything to me. I watch as a look passes between Cam and Marley, and instantly, my suspicions are raised again. Did Cam know about Carla too? Had he also kept quiet all these years?

"What? What was that?" I ask.

"What was what?" they ask in unison. Making me even more suspicious.

"That look you just gave him? Don't even think about lying to me, Marley Layton."

He looks from me to Cam, who shrugs his big shoulders from beside me.

I watch my brother rake his fingers through his brown hair, which has the first signs of grey appearing just above his ears.

"I went to see Cam."

"What?" I ask, thinking that I've asked this question a lot lately.

"The night I walked in on Maca and Carla, me and him had a long chat. He was worried that he was losing you. He had it in his head that there was something going on between you and Cam. He'd seen photos of the two of you together at Cam's club from that night you had a run in with Haley White. He felt that the way Cam looked at you in those pictures meant there might be something going on. Anyway, I told him to man up and sort his shit out, the next day, he went over to mums and the pair of you flew off somewhere on holiday, remember?"

I nod my head. "The Dominican. We stayed for two weeks."

"Whatever. Anyway, in my infinite wisdom, I thought it would be a good idea to give Cam a visit and warn him to stay the fuck away from you."

My mouth quite literally hangs open as I step back from Cam and look up at him. He holds his hands up as if he's surrendering. "Don't go blaming me for this. I told you in Australia that your mum and brothers had all threatened me with bodily harm."

He's right, he did.

But then I remember something.

"You told me he came to see you when we first got together."

Cam shrugs. "It was a little white lie. I didn't wanna cause trouble."

"Don't blame him," Marley interrupts. "I went to see him again when you came back from Australia and asked him not to mention what I'd done."

Marley tilts his head to the side and holds out his hands, palms up. "I lost ya once, George. I didn't want us falling out. I'd lost one of my best mates, I didn't wanna lose another."

I don't know whether to bitch slap or kiss him.

"Now, you got a fucking beer or what?"

I slap him.

We spend the rest of the afternoon enjoying the company of family. My brothers, their wives, some of their kids, our kids, and my parents. We eat, we drink, and we laugh. We sit around the outdoor dining table on our back patio telling stories and we reminisce. Sean's name is remembered with affection, and I neither cry nor feel guilty.

With the help of my two best friends, I've finally accepted the path that my life has taken. Having regrets is pointless. Feeling guilty changes nothing. I need to accept that what I had with Sean, was most definitely true love but it was far from perfect. The time has finally come to love my husband the way he deserves. I don't have to divide my heart into sections. It's his, all of it. He might share it with our children, Sean, and my lost babies, but he has it all.

I reach across and run my fingers through the hair at the back of his neck. I love it when he grows it longer and down past his collar.

John Legend's "All of Me" begins to play, and I smile at the relevance of my playlist again. I wonder if I actually subconsciously choose to download the songs I do?

"What are you smiling about?" Cam asks quietly from beside me. Every one seems to be engaged in their own conversations, except my parents. They are both snoring quietly, and my dad's hand is covering my mum's on the arm of her chair.

"You, Tiger. I'm smiling at you."

"And why is that, Kitten?"

"Because I love you so fucking much, that's why. I think I'm the happiest I've ever been in my life right now, and it's all thanks to you and everything you've given me."

His warm brown eyes dart over my face, giving me tingles in my belly. "Are you drunk, Kitten?"

I giggle. "Maybe a little, but that doesn't mean I don't mean every word I just said."

He nods his head slowly while rubbing his index finger back and forth over his top lip.

"So, you loving me enough for anal later?"

"Cam!" I say a little louder than I intend. "Seriously. Do you never give up?"

He shrugs his shoulders. "No."

I laugh at his honesty.

"A blow job then? Gwaaaan, you know you wanna." He winks. I melt.

"I think I can stretch to a blowie."

"Now. Go inside right now, Kitten. Go up to our bathroom and wait for me on your knees."

My mouth goes dry as my palms begin to sweat. I won't even mention what happens in my knickers.

I stand from the table, about to make up an excuse about collecting up the empties when the alarm sounds to let us know the security gates at the front of the drive are opening.

"That'll be Paige. She just text me for the gate code."

Paige hadn't made it over last night. Her new boyfriend flew in from America to surprise her, and she's bringing him over today to meet us all.

"Unlucky Tiger, the BJ will have to wait."

Cam pouts and drops his big soft bottom lip. I lean forward catch it between my teeth before kissing his mouth. I'm still holding the empty bottle of wine I'd cleared from the table a moment ago.

"Did we have odds on this one?" Marley asks.

"Yeah, I said a week at four to one, you said two days at three to one, and Cam said an hour at ten to one. Dad was being generous and gave him a month at a one hundred to one and Bailey plans on terrifying the poor bloke and gave him twenty-four hours at eleven to two."

"You lot are horrible," I tell them.

Every time one of the girls brings home a new boyfriend, my brothers, Cam, and my dad run a book on how quickly they can scare them off. It's funny, but mean.

"Just be nice for a little while, please?" Jimmie asks. "He lost his dad or step dad a few years back and now he's flown over here because his mum's really sick."

"I thought you said he was American?" Len questions.

"His dad's American, his mum's English. He's lived most of his life in the States. He's in a band I think she said, or his dad was. I can't remember, but any way, just be nice."

Marley and Bailey both clap then rub their palms together and make a *mwaaaahaha* sound.

"Bring it on," Marls says quietly and then makes an *umph* noise as Ash elbows him in the ribs.

Paige walks out onto the patio looking stunning. Her hair's piled on top of her head, she has minimum makeup on, and is wearing a pair of denim cut-offs with a gorgeous off the shoulder cheese cloth blouse in a pretty baby blue colour. The wedges on her feet matching her top perfectly. She looks every inch the catwalk model she is.

Holding her hand and looking a lot less nervous than he should, is a bloke of about twenty-five. He's wearing board shorts, a Led Zeppelin T-shirt, and a pair of flip-flops. Sunglasses cover his eyes.

"Hey, everyone. This is my boyfriend RJ. RJ, this is my family."

RJ lifts his sunglasses up to his head and rests them there.

"Hey, all, thanks for having me over." He smiles and they start to make their way towards the table. I watch them approach with a strange sense of unease creeping over me, the closer they get. There's something about this boy's face that looks vaguely familiar, and I'm not sure if it's that or the wine that is making me feel both sick and a little uncomfortable.

Marley stands abruptly, pushing his chair back noisily in the process.

He looks at me, his eyes wide with panic.

"What's the RJ stand for mate?" My dad, who is now wide awake and sizing up his next victim, asks.

"Oh, um, Rocco Junior. My dad was Rocco Taylor, it just saved on confusion."

Marley almost staggers over as he backs away from the table. I drop the empty wine bottle I was holding.

THE
END ...
FOR NOW!

PLAYLIST

"The Trouble with Us" *Chet Faker & Marcus Marr*
"History" One Direction.
"You Get What You Give" The New Radicals
"Demons" Imagine Dragons
"Can't Feel My Face" The Weeknd
"Do or Die" Thirty Seconds to Mars
"Where Love Lives" Alison Limerick
"Unbreak My Heart" Toni Braxton
"I Will Survive" Gloria Gaynor
"Second Chance" Shinedown
"Never Forget You" Zara Larsson
"7 years" Lukas Graham
"Stay With Me" Sam Smith

AUTHOR BIO

Lesley Jones was born and raised in Essex England but moved to Australia nine years ago with her family.

The Letters is her seventh book.

She has quickly gained a reputation as a writer of gritty, down to earth characters, involved in angsty and emotional plot lines. Carnage having won a number of awards for 'Best Ugly Cry'

Her readers love the fact that she can switch her stories from hot and steamy, to snot bubble crying, followed by laugh out loud moments, in the space of a few sentences.

She has described the very best part of her job is meeting her readers and already has plans to travel to the U.S for several events during 2016, a list of which can be found on her web site.

When not writing, she has admitted to being a prolific reader, getting through around four or five books a week.

She is a fan of reality TV, listening to music and watching her son play football.

Connect With Lesley @
http://lesleyjonesauthor.com/
https://www.facebook.com/LesleyJonesAuthor/
https://twitter.com/LesleyKJones
https://instagram.com/authorlesleyjones/

Find all of Lesley's books, here

lesleyjonesauthor.com

ALSO BY LESLEY JONES

CONVICTION

CHAPTER 1

I stand on the edge of the stage, eyes closed, arms raised, caught in the draft of the giant fans sitting in the wings, my hair lifts off my neck and it feels good, so fucking good. I count the beats to the final drum roll of our last song for the night... for the tour in fact and wait for the roar of the crowd as I pull my earpiece out. I open my eyes and look out across the sea of faces, arms waving in the air as Jet throws his arm over my shoulder and kisses my cheek. He's wearing a white feather boa around his neck, black leather jeans and he's shirtless and barefoot. Gunner Vance and Dom Trip, our drummer and bass guitarist join us front and centre of the stage and we all take a bow.

We're done. Eighteen months on the road is finally over. I'm going straight back to England tomorrow and I won't have to look at the ugly fucking faces of my other three bandmates until sometime next year. Well, I'll probably see Gunner at some stage as we live not far from each other, but the other two are crazy Americans and unless we have any public appearances scheduled, then naaa, I'm done travelling for a while. I'm heading home, home to England, my house, my dogs, brothers, nieces and nephews and I can't fucking wait.

A pair of knickers land at my feet as a girl screams, "Reed, take me home, take me home and fuck me." I bend my knees and shield my eyes from the house lights that are starting to come on so I can get a better look at her.

Jet leans down and says in my ear, "Get her up here, just in case the rest don't show, man."

I look up at him. "Can you see her? What's she look like?"

He shakes his head and winks at me. "I don't give a fuck. She has holes, at least three that are of interest to me, get her up here and let's get back to the room to play."

I tap the security bloke on the shoulder and point to the girl that screamed out to be fucked. I'm not sure if they're her knickers Dom now has on his head or not, but I'm sure it's not gonna be long till we find out. The giant security guard lifts the girl up over the barriers and onto the stage. She turns around to the crowd and punches the air, earning herself a massive cheer and a few boos. Jet hooks his arm over her shoulder and steers her off stage while we all follow.

No nonsense tonight, no backstage meet and greets, no fake smiles, just straight in the cars and back to the hotel to play. Gunner and Dom are both married and their wives are backstage waiting for them as we head toward the corridor. There are people hanging about everywhere and as a beer gets shoved into my hand, I pause for a second and take a few swigs.

"Mr. Reed, sorry to trouble you sir, but I wanted to give you these and wondered if you'd just take a look at them?" I lift up my sunglasses and look at the bloke standing next to me, he's more of a kid than a bloke, eighteen, nineteen at most. He has a few sheets of paper rolled up in his hand and he's holding them out to me.

"What are they?" I ask, gesturing with my chin at the paper.

"They're songs, sir. Songs that I've written. I've put my email address and cell number on the bottom. I just thought, well..." He blushes and looks down at the floor. "I'm good. What I write is good fucking shit and I just need a break. I just need someone to listen."

Fuck, I might be a prick a lot of the time but I'm not a complete arsehole, especially when it comes to kids that need a break. That was me once, all I needed was a break and Jet happened to come along and hand it to me on a plate, after he'd tried unsuccessfully to get me to suck him off that is. But once we established that wasn't going to happen, he invited me to join the band anyway, and the rest, as they say... is fucking history.

"What's your name, mate?" I ask.

"Mitch, Mitchell White. It's all on there."

I give him a wink. "Okay, Mitch Mitchell White It's All On There. I'll take these back to England with me and I'll have a look at them. If there's anything I see with potential, I'll be in touch. How's that sound?"

His eyes widen. "Seriously, you're not just fucking with me?"

Jet appears at the kid's side and runs his hand over his chest. "Ohhh, pretty new toys. For me?"

"Fuck off Harrison, your toys are waiting back at the hotel."

He folds his arms across his chest and pouts like the diva he is. I hold my hand out for the song sheets and the kid passes them to me. "Now fuck off out of here kid. There's nothing but freaky weirdo's hanging around backstage after our shows, and you're best staying well away from any of them." He nods and is gone in seconds. I turn Jet around and push him toward the exit and our limo that's waiting to take us back to the hotel with the lovely Lara, who we pulled out of the crowd earlier, already naked and sitting with her legs open on the back seat.

We climb in, close the doors, open the central console and find what we're looking for. A bottle of vodka and a nice big bag of Charlie, with six nice neat lines all ready for us on a little mirrored silver platter.

Jet sits on the leather seat next to me and we both stare between Lara's legs at her bare pussy for a few seconds.

"Top or tail?" I ask him.

"Hmmm, I might have a little taste first, then tail." The girl doesn't say a word. Jet must've told her what we like, what we expect while I was talking to the kid. Quiet, compliant, no questions asked. Just do as you're told, speak when you're spoken to and don't ever expect a rerun. What you'll get in return will be a night to remember and some mind-blowing sex that will push all your boundaries and the best orgasms and drugs of your life.

Jet lifts the mirror up to his face and snorts a line up each nostril through the platinum straw that he always carries with him. He passes the mirror to me and I hoover up my two lines quickly.

I'm about to pass it across to Lara when Jet jumps in, "Na ah man, I wanna play." He crawls on his knees over to Lara and then reaches out to me for the mirror, which I pass back to him. He tips the whole lot onto the front of her pussy. Then he just leaves it sitting there. "Put your feet up on the seat sweetheart and open those legs just as wide as you can for me."

Without saying a word, she does as she's told. Jet leans forward and licks from her arse to her clit and I watch as she shudders.

"You like that?" I ask. She looks down her body and across to me and nods.

"She tastes good Reed, you wanna try?"

Fuck that, I don't lick no chick's twat, especially one that's naked in the back of a limo ten minutes after meeting me. Ergh. Who knows who or what's been there before me? I like sex with randoms, but I have certain standards. I don't put my lips on their mouth, so there's no way I'd be putting my lips on their minge. If they want to put their lips on my dick, that's fine by me, their call. I don't make no one do anything they don't want to. I might coax, bribe or tempt but never force.

"Na, I'm good. You do what you gotta do first, dude." Without hesitation, he pushes two fingers inside her.

"Oh God," she moans as he begins to move them in and out. Her eyes are closed and her back and hips are arching off the seat. Jet looks over his shoulder and gestures for me to join him. He pulls his fingers from inside the girl and sucks on them. I think he's going back in, but instead he dips his wet fingers into the coke and starts scooping it inside her, moving his two fingers in and out as she moans and arches her back, once again lifting her arse and hips off of the car seat.

My dick's hard, now the coke's kicking in. My heart rate accelerates and I want to get involved. I reach over to the centre console and find the condoms and throw one to Jet.

"Turn her around," I order him. I sit back up on the seat opposite and undo my jeans. I pull out my cock and start to stroke myself as Lara crawls on her knees toward me. I lift her chin so she's looking me in the eye. "Jet's gonna fuck you from behind. I want to fuck your mouth while he does that. Is that all good with you?"

She shrugs her shoulders. "Can I have another line of coke first?"

I nod my head. "Just one though, he's shoved at least two lines inside you, it'll absorb through your skin soon and you'll start to feel it hit you."

She winks. "I already can. One more line and I'll be good to go for the rest of the night. I know my limits." I pass her the mirror and she lines up and snorts another hit. She's on all fours on the floor of the limo. Jet's on his knees behind her.

"Can I fuck your arse?" he asks her.

She looks over her shoulder at him. "Do you have lube?"

Jet looks up at me and gestures to the console that divides the seat in half. We use this limo company all the time, they know exactly what to provide. I search inside, find what I'm looking for and toss the tube to Jet. Then I pass him the big pink vibrator that I've also found in there.

"Wonderful." Jet winks.

Lara reaches out and takes my cock in her hand, she squeezes at the base and strokes up and down a couple of times before she flicks her tongue over my tip, pushing it into my slit as she does. My hips buck forward and my hand grips her hair. All the while, she takes me deeper down her throat. I tilt my head back on the car seat, enjoying the sensation of her hot mouth swallowing my cock as I watch Jet slide on a condom and lube up his fingers. I'm not gay or even bi for that matter. I'm not watching because I want to see, or admire his dick. I'm watching so I can tell him what to do, not that he doesn't know, he's a fucking expert but he likes to be told and I like to tell him. I have to tell him. Not just him, anyone that's involved has to be prepared for me to tell them exactly what to do. I have to be in control and I just love to push the boundaries, push people to their limits. Some are a bit resistant at first, especially if it goes against what they think is normal or right, but once you encourage them to give it a go, to just try it, they're soon lost in the moment and giving themselves over to doing all kinds of wrong.

I nod my head toward the vibrator lying on the back seat. "Turn that on and push it inside her, but I don't want her to come." Jet reaches behind him for the toy. I pull Lara's hair gently so she raises her eyes to once again meet mine. "Jet's got a toy back there with him. You happy to play?" She nods with my cock still in her mouth. "Good girl. Just yell 'shift' if you want us to stop doing anything. You got that?" She nods again. "Suck my balls into your mouth and enjoy what we're about to give ya." I nod my head at Jet and feel Lara's mouth tighten around me as he pushes the toy inside of her. "In and out slowly," I tell him. She moans and the sound vibrates around my balls, which have both now been sucked into her hot mouth. "Suck my cock back in your mouth, Lara, take it as far down your throat as you can. Jet's lubed his fingers and he's gonna slide them in your arse. You want that?" She releases my balls from her mouth and I shudder as the cool air of the limo hits them.

"I want his cock in my arse, not just his fingers. I want your cock in my cunt, his cock in my arse, Reed. Can I have that?" I stroke my fingers down her cheek and over her jaw. I love women like Lara, no bullshit, no pretending that she's little miss innocent. She knows exactly what she wants, she knows exactly what makes her feel good, and she ain't too scared to ask for it.

"Not a lot of room to manoeuvre in here. Don't worry, we'll make you feel good, then when we get back to the hotel, there'll be more people to play with and we can get you all filled up again. You can get every hole fucked if that's what you want. Would you like that?" I nod slightly to tell Jet to slide his fingers in her arse while I talk to her. Her back arches and I watch as she pushes back toward Jet.

"Oh God, yes, yes Reed, I'd like that. More Jet, I want more," her voice is ranging from high to low as Jet moves his fingers in and out of her arse.

"Suck my cock, Lara. Take it deep and then Jet will put that toy back inside you while he fucks your arse, but I want you to suck me first." I know once she comes she'll be good for nothing for a while and I'm not gonna be left hanging with a hard-on. Once I blow my load, they can blow theirs. She takes my cock back into her mouth and drags her teeth up and down the shaft. It's only just not painful, but I like it. I grip her hair and push her head down as I lift my hips. "Fuck her arse, Jet. Slide inside and make her feel good. Tell her what you're gonna do to her." I don't want to talk right now, I just want to blow down the back of her throat.

"I'm gonna fuck your arse now baby. I'm gonna fuck it hard and bury myself inside you, and while I do that, I'm gonna push this dildo deep inside your cunt. You're gonna feel so stretched and so full, they're gonna hear you come in Moscow with how loud I'm gonna make you scream. You ready for this baby?" She moans against my cock but doesn't answer him. I raise my hand to Jet, he knows exactly what that means and slaps Lara across her arse while I hold her head in place and push my hips into her face. "Answer me, Lara. You fuckin' ready for this?" I pull her by her hair and she releases my cock from her mouth with a pop.

Not breaking eye contact with me she says, "Yes, yes, Jet I'm ready." She keeps looking at me as she speaks and I just know what that look means. I'm clueless about women and emotions and how to read them, in general. But when it comes to fucking and what they want, I can read every little sigh, whimper, moan or look and I know exactly what Lara's look means right now. It's not really my thing, it triggers too many memories of what happened to my mum, but I don't mind obliging her just a little bit.

Just to be safe and to make sure I've got this absolutely right, I ask her first though, "You like that, me pulling your hair, him slapping your arse?"

She bites down on her bottom lip and nods her head. "D'ya think I'm weird?" she asks.

Jet leans forward and grabs her hair, not harshly but enough to make her turn her head. "I think your fuckin' perfect, baby. Now you just relax while I get myself inside you and when I do, I'll slap that pretty ass of yours and I'll pull your hair just the way you like it. You can forget Moscow, they'll be hearing you in Melbourne with the way we'll make you scream. Now relax baby, just relax." She turns back around to look at me. Her hand's wrapped tightly around my cock as she strokes up and down. I don't want to be in her mouth until Jet's buried inside her, just in case it hurts and she bites down on my dick. Yeah, it's happened before. Just the once, but I'm not likely to forget it.

Jet strokes his fingertips down her spine with one hand and with the other he squeezes more lube onto the bottom of her back, then uses his fingers to drag it where he needs it. He squeezes more lube into his hand and rubs it over his condom covered cock, his eyes meet mine as he does. Unlike my fine self, Jet will fuck anything with a hole. He prefers women, but if there are none available, he'll happily fuck or be sucked off by a bloke. He's told me many, many times that he'd love to be fucked by me, and I've told him just as many times it ain't gonna happen. Jet lines his cock up with Lara's arse and I watch her eyes flutter while he begins to push inside her.

"Open your eyes and tell me that feels good, Lara. We need to know you're okay. That feel good?" She opens her eyes, just as Jet must push in further, her back arches and she lets out the most animalistic moan. It's carnal, sensual, and totally erotic and I almost come in her hand.

"So good Reed, it feels so fucking good. Please let me suck you. I want to taste you." I shake my head. "Just a few more seconds and you can, but let's get you on your way first."

Jet pushes all the way inside her as I speak. I watch as his hands hold onto her hips and he begins to pump slowly into her. His eyes are on me as he bites down on his bottom lip.

"She feels good Reed, good and tight but I wish she was you. I wish this was your arse I was fucking." He doesn't take his eyes from mine. I don't get scared when he says these things anymore. I know he means every one of them, but they don't terrify me like they used to. He's my mate, I love him like a mate, but that's all. I like kinky, weird, fucked up sex, but I don't like to fuck men. I don't fancy men. I've watched two men fucking. Actually I've watched three and four men fucking and I've totally come in my hand over it, and all over a bird's face while I've watched a few times too, but it's because of the eroticism of the moment. It's watching them get off that's made me get off, it has nothing to do with the fact that they are men.

I push my cock back into Lara's mouth and push my hips up as the momentum of Jet pushing into her arse moves her forward. She pushes on the underside of my cock with the flat of her tongue, forcing it up to the roof of her mouth. She swallows and gags slightly and the sensation is almost too much. I pull on her hair and Jet takes that as a cue to slap her arse again, in turn making her moan around my cock.

"Push the toy back in, full speed, push it deep but be gentle," I tell him. Lara groans around my cock with anticipation and I watch her face as Jet follows my instructions. My eyes move from hers to Jet's, both of them are staring right at me. Lara starts to moan continuously now and the vibration feels fucking spot on. I get that all too familiar tingle at the base of my spine as my balls begin to tighten. I wrap her hair tightly in my hand and hold her head still as I lift my hips and fuck her face.

"Yes, yes Reed. Harder, fuck her harder. Oh God, I can feel that vibrator against my cock. Fuck, I'm gonna come. Come Reed, let me see your face. Fuck Reed! Fuck, I want you. I love you Reed, I fucking love you."

I shut my eyes to try and shut out Jet's voice. I know he's a sensitive soul, but I don't do all that love shit. I feel it, I write it in my songs, but that's as far as it goes for me… since her. I don't say those words out loud to anyone except my family.

My arse cheeks clench almost as tight as my balls and my dick throbs painfully as I come inside Lara's mouth. I squeeze my eyes shut tight, but it doesn't help. It doesn't keep her away. Yeah, when it's good I see stars. I get that white flash of light when I blow my load, but in amongst it all, every time, there's always a pair of blue eyes, long blonde hair and the face of an angel. My angel, Amoeba. It's been fifteen years and a whole world of hurt and fucking heartache since I last saw her. Yet, she's still there, still here, in my head, my belly and my heart and I so wish to fuck that wasn't the case.